a Kiss for Midwinter

COURTNEY
MILAN

This is a work of fiction. Names, characters, places, and incidents are the product of the author's imagination or are used fictitiously. Any resemblance to actual events, locales, or persons, living or dead, is purely coincidental.

For Dad.

Chapter One

Leicester, September 1857

"IN HER CONDITION," DOCTOR PARWINE WAS SAYING from the other side of the room, "she must particularly beware foul miasmas."

The atmosphere in the room was neither foul nor miasmic, Jonas Grantham thought, only gloomy and tense. The girl—and, unfortunately, she *was* a girl, no matter the situation she'd found herself in—sat stiffly on a chair across the room. Her hair was dark and unbound; her figure showed no sign of the changes that would shortly come to her. She didn't cry, although Jonas supposed that most girls in her situation would weep. She simply stared straight ahead, hands folded. Maybe she didn't understand what had happened to her.

He'd seen her a time or two before. He remembered her playing with the other girls just a few years ago, rolling a hoop down the street and shrieking with laughter, ribbons trailing after her.

She still looked more child than woman, but there was no hint of laughter about her now.

"Foul miasmas," the girl's mother breathed. "What are foul miasmas?"

"Miasmas," Parwine intoned, "are the cause of all disease, and are particularly noxious to…" He glanced down at the girl, and then narrowed his eyes. "To expecting mothers," he finished. "There are a number of miasmas which one must avoid. There is the *idio-kino* miasma, produced by…"

Jonas Grantham barely restrained himself from a roll of the eyes. In a matter of weeks, he was due to start his course of medical instruction at King's College in London. He'd beat out students with pedigrees from Oxford and Cambridge to win a prized three-year Warneford scholarship. He was itching for the first lecture—scheduled for the first of October at eight P.M., a mere six days and seven hours from this moment—and ignoramuses like Parwine made his hands itch all the more.

Truly, miasmas? In this modern day and age? The theory of miasmas had been conclusively disproven three years past. Only benighted fools still spouted that gibberish. But Jonas had asked to spend time with Doctor Parwine. He had an agreement in place to take over the man's practice as soon as he'd finished his education. Parwine had been most specific: He could come along, see how things were managed, but as an untutored (the older man's words) youth, he was expected to keep silent. So here Jonas stood, listening to an old man ramble on about miasmas.

"Finally," Parwine was saying, "there is the *perkoino* miasma, the cause of yellow fever—but surely you will not expose your daughter to that."

Her parents exchanged glances. "No, doctor, of course not. But what is to be done?"

The last weeks following the man about had not been totally useless. Jonas had learned a great deal about how *not* to be a physician from Parwine. The doctor maundered on and on with medical terminology that none of his patients understood, all of it supposition that had been rejected by scientific men within the last decades. It took all of Jonas's self-control—never excellent under ideal circumstances—to keep his mouth shut. He kept telling himself to respect his elders, and so far he'd managed. Barely.

Parwine frowned. "For the prevention of nausea and vomiting, which is so often associated with this delicate condition, I suggest a solution of lettuce water and prussic acid. Take it liberally and there shall be no ill symptoms. I shall leave a direction for such with the apothecary."

Jonas straightened from his post against the wall and took a step forward, before he checked himself.

He had started reading the medical texts for his course of study, had already begun to commit compounds and cures to memory. Prussic acid was a poison. Some suggested it in minute quantities for the headache; others as a palliative for cancerous growths. But for a pregnant woman? He couldn't remember reading any such thing. Still, it *could* exist. And there was that old dictum, that the difference between a cure and a poison was the dose. He bit his lip.

"But, Doctor," the father repeated, "what is to be done with my daughter? She is…she is only fifteen."

Parwine looked the girl up and down. "What do you think?" he finally said, in his quiet, gentle voice. "Treat her with Christian kindness. Now that you know what she is, quietly put her away."

The wife gasped and burst into tears. The girl's father gripped the seat, his knuckles whitening. "No," he said in denial.

The only one who didn't respond was the girl herself.

"I've seen it a hundred times," Parwine said with a shake of his head. "Once a girl is ruined, her life is over. Even if you can conceal the truth of her unfortunate state from those around her, the girl is worth nothing. Her life will follow one of two paths. If she acquires no moral sense, she will continue on in her sluttish ways, a burden of humiliation on all who know her. One of the moral diseases will shortly find her, and she will perish in ignominy."

"No." Her father's hand fell on the girl's shoulder. "No," he repeated, this time with greater certainty. "That's not going to happen to my little girl."

"Then accept the other path your daughter could tread. If there is any hint of goodness in her, her shame will consume her. She will never be loved; she will go into a decline. Likely she will die early and thus expiate her sin. There is nothing to be done at this juncture except to recognize the truth. Your daughter is already dead. It is only a matter of time until the condition manifests itself." Parwine gave the man a nod. "I can only treat the symptoms of this disease," he intoned. "There's nothing to be done about the cause—moral decay."

The father pulled a handkerchief from his pocket and dabbed angrily at his eyes. The only dry-eyed one among them was the girl. She stared across the room almost defiantly.

God *damn* that superstition. Jonas damned himself, too, for agreeing to keep silent as a condition of these visits. He hadn't chosen to become a doctor so that he could foretell the death of children. He'd been seduced by the stories—the stories of John Snow saving hundreds of lives by careful observation, of men who noticed the world around them and cared and thought, men who set aside irrationality in favor of cures supported by statistical research.

Parwine gathered up his things and motioned for Jonas to follow.

I have seen no scientific study that suggests that life is foreshortened by moral decay, he imagined himself saying to her father as he crossed the room to the exit.

Or maybe this: *Don't take the prussic acid. Whatever you do, don't take the prussic acid.*

Perhaps he might whisper a single phrase: *Don't believe a word he said.*

But he'd given the man his word. Besides—he told himself—he knew his place. He was scarcely twenty-one, hadn't even had his first lecture in medicine. He was not at the point where he should be publicly contradicting a man more than three times his age. Besides, what did he know? A little book learning was all he had. Maybe he was wrong. Maybe Parwine's experience meant he *did* know better.

All that was rubbish, and he knew it. As he left, her eyes fell on him. He didn't even know the girl's name, but his guilt made him see accusation in her gaze. *You could help me.*

Superstition, that—nobody could read thoughts from a single glance. It was his own conscience that he saw reflected in her eyes. But he didn't say anything. He didn't speak because he was young. He didn't speak because he doubted his memory of the pharmacopeia. And most thorny of all, Jonas kept his silence because Parwine had offered him his practice once he graduated.

It was the last reason he remembered in the weeks that followed when he queried one of the instructing physicians about the recommended dosage for prussic acid. Almost nothing, the man told him. And for pregnant women? Never.

For years afterward, Jonas dreamed of her eyes—those harsh, cold, accusing depths. He could have helped her.

When he finally graduated, he swore the oath of Hippocrates on Apollo the healer. But it was her face he saw when he spoke, her eyes that bored into his when he promised to do no harm.

Five years later

THE MOST UNREASONABLE NOTION JONAS EVER HAD—the nonsensical fixed point of his adult life—started from an excess of rationality. And yet at the time when it happened, everything he did made perfect sense.

He first heard the name "Lydia Charingford" on a brilliant summer day nearly five years after he'd made the rounds with Parwine. He discovered it, not because he recognized her, but because he didn't. He liked the look of her, so he asked his friend who she was after service one Sunday.

"Would you like an introduction?" Toford asked, a knowing look in his eye.

"It depends," he responded. "I'm trying to decide whether I favor round numbers or complete information."

Toford frowned. "For God's sake, Grantham, use English. What the devil do you mean by that?"

They were standing in a corner of the churchyard, looking over the crowd. It was a fine day at the end of summer, and all the ladies were wearing their loveliest—and their lightest—gowns. The young ladies had been casting welcoming glances his way throughout the rector's lengthy sermon. Jonas was young, handsome, and—with Parwine now retired—in possession of an excellent income.

Those curious, hopeful glances had made him feel very nice indeed. The breeze was refreshing, the sun was warm, and the ladies were all vying to make a good impression on him. It was a damned good time to be a man.

He was watching the ladies in return. No point in pretending he wasn't; he intended to take a wife and had only to choose her. But Toford was still staring at him in confusion.

"I mean," Jonas told him, "that during the service, I made a rank-ordered list of the ten prettiest young ladies in Leicester. I intend to speak with every one of them."

Toford nodded thoughtfully. "Good plan, Grantham, good plan. I did much the same thing last year, and see how it served me."

Mrs. Toford had teeth that were far too large. She wouldn't have ranked anywhere on Jonas's list. Jonas managed a polite murmur of approval.

"Ten, though," Toford continued. "Ten's a lot of women to speak with. You're tall. You're respectable. Why not limit yourself to three, maybe five? It's hard enough work, trying to see if *one* woman will suit you. My head hurts just thinking of the effort."

Jonas waved this off. "Yes, well. I have demanding tastes. What if number one snorts when she laughs? What if number six is untidy? What if number eight doesn't like me?"

"Doesn't like you?" Toford's brows rose. "Grantham, I think you have it all wrong." He looked around and then lowered his voice to just above a whisper. "See here," he said. "We're men. We don't have to marry. These girls, here? They've seen their sisters, their friends placed firmly on the shelf. They know their prospects if they don't catch a man. It's not their place to like or not like. It's their place to marry any way they can, and it's ours to choose."

"Be that as it may. One never knows what a woman might find off-putting. I'd rather cast my net broadly than miss altogether. And, as it happens, I have a few defects in my character."

For instance, he was fairly certain that his list of local beauties, arranged by degree of physical attractiveness, was not something that members of the opposite sex would find particularly compelling. Also, he had decided it would be best not to mention his main reason for wanting to marry—that he thought it expedient to procure a regular source of sexual intercourse without risking syphilis.

"Defects?" Toford squinted at him. "Huh. Strange, irrational creatures, women are. Miss Charingford is what number on your list?"

There was the problem. "Eleven. Well, ten, sometimes—but only some of the time. Miss Perrod is usually ten. But at some angles, in some lighting…" He shrugged. "You see my conundrum. If I want to talk to the ten loveliest young ladies, I might need to include Miss Charingford. But if I do, I'll have eleven, not ten. Both results make my hands itch." He rubbed them together, but it didn't help. That unpleasant sensation he felt in the palms of his hands was an illusion, a mere echo of that same itch somewhere in his brain.

"Maybe," Toford said, "maybe you should talk to her—not for the list, mind you, but just as a way of seeing her up close. Evaluating whether she should be included or not."

"Ah," he said in relief. "Good thinking."

Which was how he found himself walking around a park a few days later, with Miss Lydia Charingford on his arm, wondering how quickly he could extricate himself from the conversation. Closer examination revealed that she was number eleven. Most definitely eleven, with those freckles that he hadn't noticed from a distance and that too-wide smile. Furthermore, she fussed with the ribbons of her gown and responded to his conversational overtures in monosyllables.

"This is fine weather for September," he tried.

"Is it?" She stared straight ahead, her mouth pinched in a way that could have sunk her to twelve.

"Yes," he replied. "It is."

They walked on in blighted silence.

"Much has changed in Leicester since my absence," he tried again. "That's a new façade on the hat emporium, is it not?"

She didn't even look in the direction that he pointed. "Is it?" she asked.

Her terse responses brought out the devil in him. He'd not been lying when he said he had a few defects in his personality. He turned to her and spoke with no effort at politeness. "Did you know that before I spoke this sentence, you had uttered twenty percent of the words in the conversation? Now we are much closer to ten percent. It won't do, Miss Charingford. It won't do."

Beside him, she tilted her head. "Won't it?"

He clenched a fist, annoyed beyond measure. He'd used up his rather limited store of polite conversation already, and she wasn't even trying. In fact, she was looking up at him resentfully.

"I think it *will* do," she said. "I think it will do very well. I know what you are thinking, Doctor Grantham. You're thinking that I'm easy prey."

"I'm thinking that?" He wrinkled his nose.

She looked about, as if to verify that nobody was nearby. "That because you know of my faults, of what has happened to me, that I'll be susceptible to your blackmail and flattery."

"Blackmail!" he repeated in surprise.

"I don't care what you think of my *moral decay*," she hissed. "I am still alive, and I intend to remain so. I refuse to be ruined. If you try anything, you'll be sorry."

It was the look on her face that sparked his recognition—that defiant, accusing glare directed at him once more. It made him catch his breath, remembering the girl from five years ago. He'd worried about her after he left. Every time he'd seen an unwed mother or a prostitute in those intervening years, he'd wondered what horror his silence had brought to her.

The answer, apparently, was...nothing. Holding his tongue hadn't had any consequence. Because she was here, accepted by all. She'd not only survived, she'd managed to do so with her reputation intact.

And she was glaring at him. "So stop measuring me for your bed, Grantham," she told him. "You aren't going to have me."

He stared at her, collecting his confused feelings. He hadn't recognized her, but she'd recognized him—the difference between fifteen and twenty, apparently, being far greater than the difference between twenty-one and twenty-six. She was being uncivil to him on purpose. She thought—oh, God—she thought he was trying to—

"Rest easy, Miss Charingford," he said. "I wasn't attempting to seduce you. I had come to no conclusions about your virtue. I was only talking to you because you were the eleventh prettiest young lady in Leicester."

Faint dots of pink appeared on her cheeks. "Oh?" There was a dangerous tone to her voice now. "Eleven, am I?"

"That is—I mean—" He looked away. "Shite. I didn't mean to say that."

She didn't gasp at that obscenity. "Work your way on to number twelve," she snapped. "Number eleven wants nothing more to do with you."

She lifted her nose in the air—the eleventh prettiest nose in the entire town—and stalked away. He watched her go, his insides a total muddle.

She'd lived. She'd survived. Her reputation hadn't suffered. She crossed the park to another woman who had been waiting for her on a bench. Their heads bent together under their hats, black hair touching tawny honey, and then they laughed.

He'd never seen anything so vibrant, so full of life.

"Shite," he breathed again.

Her laughter seemed like a complete repudiation of the superstitions of the last century. It was a great light cast on the dark miasmas of the last century of medicine.

Live, Miss Charingford. Live.

She linked arms with her friend—a young lady who hadn't ranked at all—and strolled away.

He felt as if he'd been hit straight on with a cannon blast. One of the defects in his personality was a taste for the perverse. Being told he couldn't have something only made him want it more. And at the moment, he wanted. He wanted her very badly.

Toford came up behind him. "Well? What number is she?"

"Eleven," he answered.

"Not on the list, then." Toford shrugged.

"No." He still couldn't take his eyes off her. "No, she is. This list goes to eleven."

It was a lie. He knew it was a lie even as he said it. His rational mind, usually so predominant, kicked up a protest. He had hoped to establish his household within the next few months. And he had *really* been looking forward to securing that source of safe, regular sexual intercourse. There were literally dozens of women who would be willing to provide it—pretty ones, who actually smiled at him in encouragement instead of accusing him of seduction.

Miss Charingford didn't even want to talk to him. It made no sense to consider her.

But it was too late. Miss Lydia Charingford wasn't just *on* the list.

She *was* the list, and he hoped God would have mercy on his soul.

Chapter Two

Sixteen months later

MISS LYDIA CHARINGFORD STOOD UP FROM HER SEAT in the Nag's Head Hostelry and began to gather her things.

"Good of you, Miss Charingford," Corporal Dalling said next to her. "Very good indeed, to take on the role of secretary on such short notice."

Lydia smiled at him as she put the stopper in her bottle of ink. "I told Minnie I would be happy to take her position on the Workers' Hygiene Commission," she said. "And you deserve as much commendation as I do, filling the shoes of those who…are no longer here."

"Indeed," Dalling said, with a sober bow. "Indeed we are."

In the last month, Miss Wilhelmina Pursling—Lydia's best friend, who she missed dreadfully—had married and gone to London. Shortly thereafter, Captain Stevens—Lydia's former fiancé, who she missed not in the slightest—had been sentenced to six months of hard labor. *Good riddance.*

Lydia didn't want to think of Stevens. Instead, she blew on her notebook one last time, slipped the blotting paper between the pages, and checked the stopper on her ink.

"You're rather livelier than Miss Pursling," old Mr. Crawford said from across the way.

"And less practical," Lydia responded. "Happy Christmas, Mr. Crawford. Is your daughter coming up from Buford?"

Mr. Crawford's face creased in a smile. "Imagine your remembering a thing like that! Yes, she is coming, and bringing her little ones."

"How lovely! And why you think I shouldn't remember, I don't know. I played with Willa until I was nine. Please say I might stop by and bring a basket for her and the children. You wouldn't deny me the pleasure."

As she spoke, Lydia gathered up her things and placed them carefully in her satchel, securing the container of ink in a side pocket so that it wouldn't be jostled about. She was aware that she was humming as she did so—a rendition of "Good King Wenceslas."

Christmas was almost on them, and she couldn't have been happier. The air smelled of cinnamon and ginger. Pine boughs decorated lintels, even here at the Nag's Head. It was a time for wassail and cheer and—

"Happen we all miss your Miss Pursling—that is, the Duchess of Clermont," Crawford said softly. "Yes, my Willa would love your company."

The smile froze on Lydia's face.

Wassail, cheer, and the slight, selfish emptiness she experienced when she remembered that her best friend was no longer a mere hour's journey away, but a hundred miles distant.

But she forced her lips into a wider grin. "La, silly," she said. "I'll see her again next autumn, just as soon as Parliament lets out. How could I miss her?" If she smiled wide enough, it might fill that space in her heart. She pulled on her gloves. "Happy Christmas."

The group scattered in a shower of holiday greetings. Lydia waited until they were all gone, waving cheerfully, wishing everyone the best for the holidays.

Almost everyone. Her cheeks ached from smiling, but she would *not* look to her left. She wouldn't give him the satisfaction.

"Well," a dark voice said to her side as the door closed on Mr. Crawford, "you are chock-full of holiday spirit, Miss Charingford."

Lydia looked pointedly in front of her at the ivy-and-pine centerpiece on the table. "Why, yes," she said. "I suppose I am. Happy Christmas, Doctor Grantham."

He didn't thank her for the sentiment. He surely didn't return a polite greeting of his own. Instead, Doctor Grantham laughed softly and her spine prickled.

Lydia turned to him. He was tall—so very much taller than her that she had to tilt her neck at an unnatural angle to stare him down. His eyes sparkled with a dark intensity and his mouth curled up at one corner, as if he nursed his own private amusement. He was handsome in a brooding sort of way, with those eyes, that strong, jagged nose. All the other girls giggled when he looked their way. But Grantham made Lydia remember things she didn't like to think about.

He particularly made her remember them now. He looked at her down his nose and gave her a faint, mocking smile, as if she'd made a terrible error by offering him holiday greetings.

Lydia straightened. "Happy Christmas," she repeated, her voice tight. "You're allowed to say it back even if you don't *really* wish the other person happy. It's a polite nothing. I won't imagine you mean anything by it—just as you know that I don't truly care whether you're happy."

"I didn't think you were wishing me happy," Grantham responded. "I thought you were simply describing events as you saw them. Tell me, Miss Charingford, is it *really* a happy Christmas for you?"

Lydia flushed. Christmas memories were not always fond. In fact, Christmas brought to mind the worst moments in her life. Leaving home with her parents and her best friend six years earlier. A dingy house let in Cornwall, and that awful, awful night when the cramps had come…

"Yes," she said forcefully. "Yes, it is. Christmas is a time for happiness."

He laughed again, softly—mockingly, she thought, as if he knew not only the secret that she kept from all of Leicester, but the one she held hidden in her heart. He laughed as if he'd been there on that dreadful night that had seemed the absolute opposite of Christmas—an evening when a girl who was very much not a virgin had miscarried. There'd been blood and tears rather than heavenly choirs.

"You," he said to her, "you of all people…you should relent from this incessant well-wishing." He shrugged. "You *do* know that it doesn't make any difference, whether you wish me well or I wish you happy."

Lydia's eyebrows rose. "Me, of all people?" He'd so closely echoed her thoughts. Sometimes, it seemed as if he knew precisely what she was thinking—and when he spoke, it was designed to make her feel badly. Lydia bared her teeth at him in a smile. "What do you mean by that? Have I less of a right to good cheer than the average person?"

"Less of a right? No. Less of a reason, however…"

"I couldn't know what you intend by such veiled assertions."

His eyes met hers, and he raised one sardonic eyebrow. "Then let me unveil them. I am, of course, referring to the man who got you with child while you were one yourself."

She gasped.

"I am always astonished, Miss Charingford, when you manage to have a happy word for any member of my sex. That you do—and do it often— never ceases to amaze me."

The room was empty but for them, and he stood two feet from her. He'd spoken quietly, and there wasn't the least danger of their being overheard. It didn't matter. Lydia balled her hands into fists. The smile she'd scarcely been able to form moments before was forgotten entirely.

"How dare you!" she hissed. "A *gentleman* would do his best to forget that he knew such a thing."

He didn't seem concerned at all with her accusation. "But you see, Miss Charingford, I must be a doctor before I allow myself to be a gentleman. I do not recall such a thing in order to hold you up for moral condemnation. I state it as a simple medical fact, one that would be relevant to further treatment. Certain female complaints, for instance—"

Lydia bristled. "Put it out of your mind. You will never treat me as a patient. *Ever.*"

Doctor Grantham did not look put out by this. Instead, he shook his head at her slowly, and gave her a smile that felt…wicked. "Ever?" he asked. "So if you're trampled by a runaway stallion, you'd expect me to express my wholehearted regrets to your parents. 'No, no,' I will say. 'I couldn't possibly stop your daughter from bleeding to death on the cobblestones—my professional ethics forbid me to treat anyone who has unequivocally refused me consent.'"

He was laughing at her again. Well, technically, he wasn't *actually* laughing. But he was looking at her as if he wanted to, as if he couldn't wait for her to scramble and reverse her prior edict. Lydia gave him a firm nod instead. "That's exactly right. I would rather bleed to death than have your hands on me." She tucked her gloves under her arm and reached for her shawl.

He was still smiling at her. "I'll pay my respects at your funeral."

"I don't want you there. If you dare come, I'll haunt you in your sleep."

But that only sparked a wicked gleam in his eye. He took a step closer, forcing her to tilt her head up at an unnatural angle. He leaned over her, bending his neck. And then he whispered.

"Why, Miss Charingford." That smile of his tilted, stretching. "There's no need to wait until you're *dead* to visit my bed. In fact, I'm available right now, so long as we finish before—"

She didn't think. She pulled back her arm and slapped him as hard as she could—slapped him so hard that she could feel the blow reverberating all the way back to her shoulder.

He rubbed his cheek and straightened. "I suppose I deserved that," he said, somewhat ruefully. "Your pardon, Miss Charingford. I was in the wrong. I should never have spoken that way." He looked down. "In my defense—and I know this is a weak defense—we were talking about death, and that always brings out the worst of my humor. Which, as you have no doubt discovered, is abominable to begin with. I pray that I do not one day watch you bleed to death on the streets." His voice was solemn, and for once, that twinkle vanished from his eyes. "I hope it is not you. But it will be someone."

For a moment, she felt a tug of sympathy. To deal with death every day, to have only humor to keep the specter of darkness at arm's length... But then she remembered everything he had said to her—those pointed reminders that she was a fallen woman. She remembered his all-too-knowing eyes, following her across the room whenever she encountered him. She might have been able to forget her mistake for months on end were it not for him.

She wound her scarf around her neck. "Now you've made me regret striking you."

"Truly?" That eyebrow rose again.

He stood close, so close that when she picked up her coat, he was able to intervene and hold it out for her. Nice of him to act the gentleman *now*, now when it meant that she sensed the warmth of his hands against hers, his bare fingers brushing her wrist. His touch should have been cold like his depraved, shriveled heart. Instead, a jolt of heat traveled through her.

"Truly." She set her hat on her head and adjusted the cuffs of her coat to cover her gloves. "You see, I interrupted you before you told me how long you were giving yourself to finish the deed. I'd not have given you above thirty seconds, myself."

His crack of laughter followed her out the door. She could hear it echoing in her mind—laughter that sounded jolly and fun, without a hint of meanness to it, the kind of laughter she would expect to hear next to the sprightly ring of Christmas bells. It wasn't fair that Doctor Jonas Grantham of all people could laugh like that. Still, she heard it playing in her mind—saw him, his head thrown back, delighted—until the windswept streets swallowed up the sound of his merriment.

Chapter Three

IT WAS NOT TO HIS COMFORTABLE BELVOIR STREET HOME that Jonas went after the meeting. He had a much longer journey—up Fosse Road, picking his way carefully across paving stones that were slick with ice. The houses became smaller the further he went from the center of town: shoved together in a row, shrinking from three- and four-story stone affairs to squat two-story cottages fronted by brick walls that enclosed only enough room for the most meager kitchen gardens.

The only break from those small, depressing abodes was a space of dry dirt, ringed by a low stone wall. In summer, it served as a park where the children might play. In winter, with the weather so cold, it usually stood vacant. A rough structure had been erected several years ago in the middle, little more than a stage with a roof and three walls surrounded by wood benches. It was used for the occasional gathering—mostly amateur productions put on by the children. The structure surrounding the stage had been plastered over long ago, making it an unrelieved dingy white breaking up the monotony of the dirt.

Today, though, he saw a few men setting up a tree on the stage, one so large that it scarcely fit under the roof. It was a monster, maybe fifteen or sixteen feet high, and the sound of laughter rang out as the men hauled it erect.

Yule logs and holly, the traditions of Jonas's childhood, had fallen out of fashion in favor of new German practices popularized by the late Prince Albert. To his eye, the tree seemed overlarge, a towering presence that demanded attention. By the time the tree was decorated with glass bugles and quilled stars, it would have transformed this space into something that felt alien. It left him feeling oddly disconnected from the upcoming holiday. Maybe it would still be Christmas if there were trees instead of ivy, if Boxing Day were replaced with visits from Kris Kringle, but it didn't seem the same to him.

It would never be the same, not without his father ringing a string of bells at his bedroom door at six in the morning. Not without his father putting his mittens on and dragging him out-of-doors to examine the snow—if there was any—or to show him the countryside. This Christmas promised none of the things he remembered from childhood. His father couldn't get out of bed any longer, and Jonas wasn't sure he could bear hearing the bells, knowing that his father wasn't ringing them. He turned his head away from the tree—from the men who hauled it erect, and the women who looked on, passing out steaming mugs amidst much laughter. They were thirty feet away, but it might as well have been a mile.

The house he was looking for stood on the far corner. A trickle of smoke issued from the chimney. The garden in front was nothing but mud, stones, and a few decrepit weeds. As Jonas opened the iron gate, he looked for some sign of life aside from the smoke. But the curtains, as always, were drawn shut.

He bent, picked up a crumpled paper that had blown inside the gate, and balled it up for future disposal.

So doing, he knocked on the door.

As always, the reply was minutes in coming.

The paper was wet and dirty and his hands were cold. His hands were perpetually cold these days; he chafed them together for warmth, but remembered at the last moment that he wasn't supposed to blow on them. He was about to knock again when the door finally opened.

The smell always struck him first. It was an earthy, musty scent, the smell of dank places hidden from sunlight, of air that sat still and unmoving. It always took him a few breaths before he grew used to the odor.

"Good evening, Henry," Jonas said. "He's here, I take it?"

He could scarcely see the figure at the door, so dark was the interior. Henry was a silhouette, scarcely five feet tall, skinny and slouched.

"Aye," Henry said, moving back. "Where else would he be?"

Jonas spread his hands—his cold hands—in supplication to the universe and looked up. "Where else," he sighed, "indeed."

Every time he came here, he told himself that it couldn't possibly get any worse. Every time he returned, he was proven wrong.

The front room—could one even call it a *room* when there was no room at all?—was completely filled. A little bit of illumination beckoned; a hint of reflected fire filtered down a narrow hallway.

It *looked* like a narrow hallway, at a first glance. At a second glance, one might have concluded that the walkway was a natural tunnel made in some underground cave. The walls seemed like jagged, discontinuous rocks.

It was only when one got close that one could see that this cavern was not made of limestone. It was made of discarded bits of furniture, old copper pots that had been broken and tossed in the midden. There were curving pieces of iron that looked to have been taken from the broken wheels of carts and barrels that had been staved in. These were all stacked together precariously. Dimly, he recognized the newest article to join the collection: an old stove, its boiler ruptured. It added a faint metallic rustiness to the bouquet of the room.

"Henry," Jonas said, "you realize that to get to the bedroom, I'll have to actually scuttle sideways at this point."

The silhouette of Henry shrugged in the darkness.

"There is no room for anything else. You'll have to tell him there's no room, the next time someone brings something by. He must stop buying rubbish."

Another shrug. "That's what you said last time. But actually, if you can shove some of the smaller things over the barrels, there's still nearly a foot of good space there."

"Of course. Over the barrels." Jonas rubbed his forehead. "And pray it doesn't cause an avalanche. It doesn't matter. Whether there's space now doesn't matter."

Henry shrugged again. "If I tell him he can't, he's going to sack me like he did the others."

Maybe it wasn't as bad as it looked. Maybe...

Jonas knew he had failures enough, and a tendency to too much neatness and order was one of them. His fingers twitched if he saw a single picture frame skewed out of alignment. The disorder of this house gave him a full-body itch, one that settled just beneath his temples and could not be relieved.

He picked a few spoons off the floor as he made his way through the wreckage and set them, neatly in order, atop a metal box. It felt as if he were trying to close a mortal wound with two inches of twine.

The back room was, thank God, not quite so dire. That only meant that the rubbish that ringed the walls had only reached head-height, and that the area around the fireplace was mostly clear. There were a few boxes filled with grimy bits of metal strewn about. But at least there was a basin and soap and a table where a boy like Henry might prepare a simple meal.

Jonas washed his hands before heading up the stairs.

When he'd been young, there had always been rubbish around. Inevitable, really, when your father was a scrap-metal dealer. But it had been carefully sorted then, and had been kept in the sheds out back and the scrap-yards. Most importantly, the piles of scrap had left as swiftly as they had come in. But his father's health had begun to fail, and he'd gradually stopped selling. He'd stopped selling, but he hadn't stopped taking things in. By the time Jonas had finished his final year at King's College, matters had come to this point.

He made his way up the stairs into the top bedroom. The steeped roof was low enough over the staircase that he had to stoop until he came into the center of the room. There was a second fireplace here, and a nice fire of coals burning. Mr. Lucas Grantham sat up in bed and was squinting at the stairwell.

"Well?" he demanded. "What have you got?"

Jonas spread his hands out. "It's me, Father."

"Hmmph." The man folded his arms, tucking his hands into his armpits. "Well, don't be long," he groused. "I'm doing business today, I am."

Jonas looked around the room doubtfully. "I...see."

A wooden box was set up on one side of the bed, filled with chunks of rusting metal. At the foot, bits of splintered wood and paper were scattered about.

"Got some old barrels just yesterday," his father said. "Good fastenings in those, if you know what to look for. Made my first fortune in fastenings, looking for those little bits of metal that other men couldn't be bothered to find."

Jonas looked around for a chair, but either the one that had been here yesterday had been dismantled for its nails, or it had been swallowed by the rubbish that crowded the north side of the room, spilling onto the floor.

"That's how I won your mother, it was. Fastenings." He made a happy noise.

Jonas settled himself gingerly on the edge of the bed. "Father," he said. "You don't have to do this any longer."

Once, Mr. Grantham had owned a regular scrap-metal empire. He'd traded not only in fastenings, but in larger pieces—obsolete machinery from the factories, iron rails from train tracks that had fallen out of use, purchased at cut rates from bankrupted railways. He'd always been scrupulously frugal—one of Jonas's earliest memories was his father plucking a horseshoe nail from the middle of the street, ignoring the filth it stood in, while Jonas stood three feet away and prayed desperately that none of the other boys would see him. But this...this was different.

"'Course I do," his father replied. "Always have. Always will. Never too late to save a penny. I've got to do it." He glared at Jonas. "I know what you're about, boy—want nothing more than to have me dependent on you, dancing to your tune. But this is my livelihood, boy. Nobody's taking it away."

"I'd have no objection, if you sold what you took in. But—"

"As soon as I'm feeling well again, I'll start up once more," Mr. Grantham replied.

"It's been over a year. And you've enough money in the bank, there's no need to worry."

"A year? Faugh," Mr. Grantham grumbled. "It's been a few weeks at most, and I'm feeling better already."

That was one of the things that had begun to go wrong. In the first few days after his father's heart attack, he'd seemed confused and stricken. But he'd survived, and even if Lucas found himself short of breath most of the time, Jonas had harbored hope. That hope died more everyday. It wasn't just his father's body that was failing, but his mind. His sense of time had melted away. He no longer remembered that it had been months since he was able to leave the bed. And he'd focused on bringing in scrap iron, more and more of it. Perhaps some part of him believed that if he could only bring in enough, if he could fill is home with the rubbish that had made up his past, that the future wouldn't come.

Jonas had tried everything. One time, he'd even hired a pair of men to go in and forcibly clear the house. But his father had shrieked and carried on. He'd called for the police, in fact, and when they had come, they had regretfully informed Jonas that as it was Mr. Grantham's house, and as he did in fact own the rubbish, it would be theft if Jonas removed it.

That had been a lovely day, his father threatening to have him prosecuted if he continued. Now, he simply tried not to upset the man.

At this point, Jonas could have recited the relevant section in Conolly's *Indications of Insanity* from memory. "Where the individual has always been eccentric, the eccentricity will probably be increased by age. For one unacquainted with the previous habits of the patient, he may seem to be mad, although, perhaps, merely a humorist, who has in declining life become a little more childish in his humors." Mr. Grantham was still the same man he'd always been—a little dour, a little suspicious, and extremely frugal. It was just that those qualities had been refined over and over until he could think only of scrap and scrap metal, until his home had become a veritable midden, with himself appointed as King of Rubbish.

All Jonas had to do to stop this was to have his own father declared incompetent.

"You'd be married by now, I wager," his father said, "and giving me grandchildren already—if only you still saved fastenings." This was said with a sad air. "Now you're all alone."

Jonas might once have pointed out that he was twenty-six years old— that his father had married far later than he, that he might still have his choice of a dozen women. But there was some truth in what his father said.

Oh, not the folderol about fastenings. As for the rest...

He could have been married last year, but for his fascination with Lydia Charingford.

The mornings when he tipped his hat to her on the street were always the brightest. He smiled when he saw her. He saw so little hope in the world, and she saw far too much. There were days he wanted to sit and watch her, to figure out where all that good cheer came from.

He knew he tended toward gloom. It made him consider blood poisoning and heart attacks when someone else might see a touch of indigestion. Those carefully considered worst-case scenarios made him a good doctor, but they also made him feel like a dark little raincloud.

When Lydia Charingford was around, though, he felt like a *smiling* dark little raincloud. He liked the way she saw things, even as she baffled him. He liked the way she saw all the world…except the portion of it that contained him.

He was the one person she didn't like. He should have given up.

But every once in a while, he'd catch her eye by accident, and the blush on her face when she turned away… That alone had kept him from moving on.

He knew he should have said something—something other than stray, blunt remarks that never turned out well—but it was difficult to talk to a woman who always thought the worst of him. Besides, she'd become engaged to Captain Stevens six months ago, and Jonas wasn't the sort of man who would encroach where he had no right.

Months had gone by. He'd called himself a fool. In love with another man's fiancée? Now that had been truly insupportable. But then she'd ended the engagement.

"You're right about that," he said to his father. "It's time I made up my mind on that front. I don't suppose you'd agree to clean this place out if I married within the year?"

"Clean this out?" his father echoed, looking about him. "I suppose I will, at that."

Jonas looked up sharply. "You will?"

It was time—past time—to attempt to win her over, notwithstanding all the many defects in his personality. His father's agreement on this score was all that he had been waiting for. If he succeeded, she'd make him happy. And if he failed…it was long past time for him to choose someone else.

"'Course I will," his father said. "I told you, the only reason it's piling up a little now is that I'm not on my feet. Once I'm well again, I'll take care of it all."

Jonas sighed, and judged that promise to be as worthless as the junk that spilled out of boxes around him. "Of course you will," he said, looking upward. He'd been hearing that from his father every day for the last year, and every day, he could mark another sign of his increasing fragility. "Of course you will."

"WELL, MISS CHARINGFORD," JONAS SAID, "I suppose you're wondering why I'm here."

Miss Charingford traced the edge of her scarf with her finger. It could no longer be called a morning sun, that brilliant light that spilled through the plate glass window in the front parlor of her parents' home, but it was only just past noon. The light kissed the face of the eleventh prettiest woman in all of Leicester, and Jonas felt jealous.

But she didn't look at him. She simply shrugged. "Not at all, Doctor Grantham," she said. "I'm not wondering. Wonder requires thought; thought requires concern." She looked over at him and raised one eyebrow.

"And concern, Doctor Grantham, requires me to care about your motives in the first place."

Which I do not. She left that implied, but unspoken.

"I am constantly amazed by you," he said. "To say that you view the world through rose-colored glasses would be the greatest of understatements. You don't just see things tinted in pink; you see a world that is pink all the way through."

She gave him a tight, forced smile.

"When I push you on it, you don't simper or fluster or make excuses. You defend what you see with a surprising capacity for logic."

"A *surprising* capacity," she said flatly. "My, the compliments you give a woman. Do say on."

Jonas felt himself flush. He had, in fact, intended it as a compliment. "That came out poorly. I only meant that you see the entire world in glowing terms. The entire world, that is, except for me."

Miss Charingford didn't look at him. In fact, Jonas rather thought she was avoiding his eyes altogether. Her fingers flexed. "I don't see the world in glowing terms, Doctor Grantham. I theorize, and not all my theories are positive."

"I don't believe that for one second."

"Of course *you* don't," she said. "But I allow myself to consider both the good possibilities and the bad. I merely choose to focus on the good, when it's there to be found."

"Do you?"

"You, on the other hand, are only aware of the bad." She looked away.

"I hardly think you know me well enough to judge that," he replied mildly.

"Well enough. Take me, for instance."

He would like to, actually. He would have liked to take her very much. But he turned to her and gestured attentively.

"You think that because I am optimistic, I am frivolous and foolish—a veritable lily of the field, unable to toil, spin, or read the *London Quarterly* when the opportunity arises." She leaned in and whispered. "Let me tell you a secret. I'm not stupid."

"Actually, Miss Charingford," he said, inclining his head toward her, dropping his voice as low as he could. "I already knew that about you. I have never thought you stupid. Or foolish. Or ignorant." He set his hand atop hers. "Just different."

Her breath caught and her eyes widened. She glanced down at his fingers—he could feel her knuckles against the palm of his hand.

"You surprise me because you know precisely the same things that I know, and you come to the exact opposite conclusions," he said. "Every time you open your mouth, I'm convinced that you must be the most naïve girl on the face of the planet. And yet…" He shook his head. "And yet every time you open your mouth, you demonstrate that you are not."

He hadn't moved his hand the entire time. She sat, looking up into his eyes, and he felt positively mesmerized. Her eyes were so dark, her skin so fair. Her hair was put up, with little ringlets escaping from the knot to fall at her cheek.

Miss Charingford always dressed well. There was a sleek attention to detail in her toilette that even his fashion-ignorant brain could identify. But today, dressed in a russet gown that highlighted the pink of her cheeks, she looked particularly adorable. Those light freckles dusting across her nose practically begged to be touched.

She pulled her hand from underneath his, balling it into a fist at her side. "That is because, as I said, I see both the good and the bad in everything that comes my way. That way, I am never unprepared." She shot him a look, one that had him swallowing. "Around you, I need a great deal of preparation."

"Ah. So you might not *wonder* about why I have come. But perhaps you've theorized about it."

She pressed her lips together and looked away. "It wouldn't be polite to say."

"The one thing we have never been to one another is polite. But never mind, Miss Charingford, I shall fill in the bad and the good. Either I am an unspeakably rude fellow, the kind who vents his ire and spleen on perfectly innocent young ladies, or…" His gaze slid to her profile. She was still looking across the room, refusing to meet his eyes. "Or," he said softly, "I am madly in love with you. And I have been for this last year."

His heart seemed to stop in his chest as he spoke. The seconds that should have ticked by froze into an agony of waiting, watching to see if her eyes would widen. If she would turn to him and see the truth writ large on his features. If she would even care.

But she didn't look at him. He couldn't read what he saw in her expression—a tightening of her jaw, a tensing of her hand before she pressed it flat against the table.

"Well," she finally said, "you're doing it wrong. You are supposed to pick two possibilities—one dreadful and one lovely." She turned then, deliberately meeting his eyes. There was a spark of merriment in them. "Confess, Doctor Grantham. That's *two* dreadful ones."

It was such a curious sensation, that constricting feeling that settled about him. He felt as his heart were made of green bottle-glass—cold and wavy, distorting the light that passed through it until even the brightest emotion was stripped of all illumination. He pushed the corners of his lips up into a smile.

"Ah, Miss Charingford. You slay me."

Maybe some hint of the truth leaked out, because the light faded from her eyes, and she peered up at him. "I didn't hurt your feelings, did I? I meant it—"

"In all good fun," he said brusquely. "Yes."

Fastenings, he could imagine his father saying. *I wooed your mother with fastenings.* Jonas tried to imagine Miss Charingford's face if he presented her with a horse-shoe nail retrieved from some mucky boulevard. She would probably look at him...approximately as she looked now, as if he'd offered her a bouquet ripe with horse-droppings.

He'd done it to himself. He had a dreadful sense of humor, a too-blunt tongue, and he'd never seen the point in holding either back. But she'd never take him seriously now. He had told her outright that he loved her, and she hadn't seen it as anything but another volley, another ill-considered jest. The entirety of his feelings had become a joke. She didn't even see him as a friend, let alone a suitor.

If he were another person entirely, he might burst into flowery speech. If he did, she'd probably laugh at him. Besides, he didn't believe in pretending to be anyone other than who he was. Even if she swooned at whatever poetic nonsense he managed to spout, she would only be disappointed once they grew comfortable with each other and he went back to making jokes about death and gonorrhea.

"Don't worry, my dear," he said, a little more brusquely than he'd intended. "I'm a doctor. We're not allowed to have feelings; they interfere with our professional judgment. I'm here to make you a proposition."

"Oh?" Her jaw squared. "On a scale of boring to improper, where does it fall?"

"Mildly scandalous." He tapped the table. "I have a wager for you, if you've the stomach for it."

Up went her chin again. "There's no point to a wager," she said. "There is nothing you have that I could want."

He ignored this. "I wager," he said, "that I could show you a situation before Christmas that would be beyond even your capacity for good cheer."

She frowned. "What do you mean?"

"I see the worst of Leicester. In five minutes, I'll leave for my next appointment. You smile and you wish and you see an entire world set forth in the most optimistic terms. I wager that I can find you a situation that lacks a bright side."

He didn't have fastenings, but he did have his version of it—house calls.

She mulled this over for a few moments. "What do you get if you win?"

"We'll get to that in a moment, if you please. The more salient question is, what would you wish if you win? You could ask me for any favor. You could make me stand on my head in the market square for twenty minutes, if you wanted. Think, Miss Charingford, of all the ways you might humiliate me. Surely that would be worth *something* to you."

She frowned and tapped her fingers against her lips. She didn't look at him as she thought; she just tilted her head and narrowed her eyes. Finally, she gave a nod. "What if I said I wanted you never to talk to me again?"

His lungs stopped working. "That's…that's what you'd want?"

"No sarcastic comments. No biting wit. No reminders of my past mistakes." Her voice dropped. "Yes, Doctor Grantham. That would tempt me. That would tempt me greatly."

He swallowed. Every word she spoke hurt. She didn't just dislike him. She hated him. But if that was the way of things… Best that he discover it now.

"What if you changed your mind later? Would I be barred from speaking?"

She considered this a moment. "I suppose that if I should lose my head so far as to want to hear the grating tones of your voice once more, I should be allowed the opportunity to reverse the wager. It needn't be a permanent condition." She tilted her head at him. "It will be, of course."

"Unless I win."

She waved off that possibility. "And what humiliation will you heap on me if you should prevail?" Miss Charingford asked.

"I want a kiss."

Her head turned to his. Her eyes widened. She looked into his gaze. He wanted to reach out and touch the tips of his fingers to her cheek, to graze his hand down the line of her jaw until her lips softened.

"A kiss," she repeated. "You want a kiss. From *me.*"

"Your ears appear to function with tolerable accuracy." His own words seemed harsh and clipped. "If you fail, I get a kiss from you. An honest kiss, mind—not some shabby peck on the cheek."

As he spoke, her eyebrows raised. Her lips thinned. "Do you think me loose, Doctor Grantham?"

"I think you as loose as a citadel. Why else would I have stooped to making elaborate wagers with you in exchange for the smallest token of your affections?"

She didn't seem to hear that. Instead, her brow furrowed and she looked up. Finally, she nodded to herself as if she'd solved a difficult problem. "I see what you're about, Grantham. You think to teach me a lesson. You want to show me that the world is more frightening—and more dark—than I believe."

"Maybe I'm simply looking for an excuse to spend time in your company." Maybe he wanted her to see him outside the social settings where he performed so poorly. He wanted a chance for her to see *him,* a chance to break through the impossible wall of her dislike. "Maybe," he said, "I'm thinking that the days are dark and long, that midwinter is approaching. Maybe, Miss Charingford, all I really want is a kiss."

If she reached the end of their time together and felt any affection for him at all, she'd never enforce that ridiculous forfeit that she'd asked for. If he won, he'd get to kiss her. And if she didn't like him after spending time in his company...

Yes, it was definitely preferable to realize it now.

"The more I think on it," he said, "the more I realize that it is impossible for me to lose."

"We have more than two weeks until Christmas, and I refuse to shadow you the entire time. Will three visits suffice, do you think?"

Three visits. They'd walk to the calls and back. That might amount to a handful of hours in her company. If he couldn't convince her to consider him in that time, it was never going to happen.

"Three visits will do." He paused. "If you're accompanying me on house calls at Christmas time, you might consider..."

"I'll make a basket," Miss Charingford said. "Of course I will."

"Tomorrow, then, we'll be going to see a woman who has eight children and one more on the way." He looked over at her. "Bring something appropriate."

Chapter Four

THERE WAS A TRADITION THAT HAD BEGUN SIX YEARS AGO, one that was always important to Lydia. These days, she never felt as if Christmas were coming until she'd decorated her father's office.

Another man might have frowned and ordered her out of the room as he bent over the account books. But then, Lydia had always been aware that her father was rather out of the ordinary.

He sat at his desk as she wound red ribbon about the base of the oil lamp that stood on a side table. He didn't look up at her. He didn't say a word. Still, when she cut the fabric and began to add holly, he leaned over and, almost absentmindedly, squeezed her hand.

"Can I get you anything?" she asked. "Tea? A glass of wine?"

"Mmm," he replied. "A one. I'm missing a one."

She peered over his shoulder. "You left it on the last page," she said after a moment's study. "When you carried the amount over."

He looked up at her, peering over the rims of his glasses. "Did I, then?"

She ran her finger down the facing page and pointed.

He frowned—not a real frown, that; she knew his moods well enough to know when he was unhappy. And right now, he wasn't. "So I did," he said. "So I did."

But instead of returning to his books, he looked at her—at the heavy gown of dark rose she'd donned, so unsuited for an afternoon at home.

"You're going out," he said mildly.

She shrugged, feeling suddenly awkward. Lydia knew for a fact that she could tell her father anything. She'd told him about that dreadful ordeal with Tom Paggett, after all. Her father knew the absolute worst about her, and he loved her anyway. She didn't understand why.

And she didn't want to tell him about her wager with Doctor Grantham. He trusted her, and even though she knew why she'd agreed—for no reason other than to rid herself of him—she was aware that the situation might have appeared somewhat improper if she were to reveal the stakes.

A kiss? From Grantham? The very idea made her shiver. No, it had made perfect sense to make sure that Grantham never talked to her again. She'd never have to feel that nervous anticipation creeping up her spine. All she had to do was endure him for a few afternoons, and she'd be free of him.

"I am going out," she said awkwardly.

He glanced down, caught a glimpse of her half boots. "Going out walking. With a man?"

Lydia made a face. "Not a man," she muttered. "At least—not like that."

Even though there was nothing exceptional in walking with a gentleman, another father—knowing what he did of Lydia—would have restricted her movements, refusing to let her do what the other young ladies did. He might have told her she was no longer trustworthy.

Mr. Charingford was not those other fathers. When Lydia had told her father she was pregnant, he'd held her close for many long minutes, not saying a word. He'd called her mother in, leaving Lydia in her comforting embrace. Then he'd left the house. She had no idea what he'd said or done, but Tom Paggett had left town two days later. Her father didn't speak much, but she'd never doubted him.

One of Lydia's first memories was playing on the floor of her father's study. Her nurse had darted in, grabbing her up with a flood of apologies and a scold for Lydia.

"Can't you see your father's busy?" she'd remonstrated.

But her father had simply shrugged. "If you take her away every time I'm busy," he'd said placidly, "I'll never see her. She can stay."

He'd not been too busy to take her to Cornwall when she was pregnant, hiding her condition from those who would have disparaged her. And on Christmas morning, when she'd not been sure if she would live, he'd come into her room with ribbons and holly. He hadn't said a word; he'd only set them around the room, fussing with ribbons he scarcely knew how to tie because he'd wanted to do something.

Sometimes, when she thought of her father, she felt as if there were something vast and impossibly large inside his slight frame, something too big for words. It certainly felt too big for *her*.

And so now, she put ribbons in his study as Christmas approached. It was the only way she could return those too-large emotions.

"You're not walking out with a man?" His tone was congenially suspicious. He looked pointedly at her.

So it was her favorite walking dress, the one she saved for special occasions. He'd seen her altering the trim last night, replacing the light blue cuffs with two inches of white linen that she'd embroidered herself.

Lydia felt herself flush. "I like looking well, no matter who I'm with." She wasn't even sure why she'd dressed with such particular care. Maybe she just didn't want to give Grantham another opportunity to poke fun at her.

"Mr. Charingford. Miss Charingford." A maid ducked her head in the doorway, interrupting the conversation.

Behind her stood the tall figure of Jonas Grantham. His coat was slung over one arm; he held a large black bag in the other.

"You see?" Lydia sad. "Not a man. A doctor."

Grantham looked to one side, biting his lip, and her father raised an eyebrow at her.

"That's not what I meant," Lydia muttered.

But her father simply took off his spectacles and set them on his desk

Grantham didn't look at her. "I believe what your daughter meant was that she agreed to accompany me on a call to the Halls, out by Lipham Road."

"Halls, Halls." Her father frowned. "Do I know these Halls?"

"It's unlikely. She takes in laundry," Grantham said. "Her husband died, leaving her with sole responsibility for eight children. When we spoke at the Workers' Hygiene Commission, Lydia agreed to bring the Halls a basket for the coming holidays."

Her father glanced over at Lydia with a small smile on his face.

"It will be a perfectly unremarkable visit," Grantham said. "Public streets the whole way there, and Mrs. Hall there to chaperone your daughter once we enter the building."

"Is that what you were working on this morning?" her father asked. "Putting together a basket for this Mrs. Hall?"

Lydia nodded.

Her father fixed Doctor Grantham with another look. "Well, Doctor, despite my daughter's protestations, you do appear to be a man. A word with you, if you please."

Doctor Grantham stepped into the office; with a jerk of his head, her father motioned for Lydia to leave. She sniffed and swept out, shutting the door behind her. It didn't stop her from standing on the threshold though, and setting her ear to the door.

"So," her father aid without preamble. "You're walking out with my Lydia." His tone left little doubt as to what he meant by those words.

She waited to hear Grantham deny the implication—that he had some sort of romantic interest in Lydia. But if he made an audible response, she could not hear it.

Whatever he said—whatever gesture he made—her father grunted. "Yes, yes," he said, "I understand. But I want to make something clear. If you hurt my daughter by word or by deed…"

"Mr. Charingford," Doctor Grantham said, "first, do no harm. Those are not just words I mumbled so that I could get a few fancy letters before and after my name. They are a belief. I don't hurt people. I intend harm to your daughter least of all."

Lydia pulled back, a little puzzled, and stared at the door. She'd expected Grantham to make some sort of caustic comment about how the damage to Lydia had already been done. But she'd not even heard a note of sarcasm in his voice.

"She's far more delicate than she looks," her father was saying. "Don't think you can talk to her in your usual way. She's sensitive and—"

"Your daughter," Grantham replied, "is stronger than you think. I wouldn't be taking her to see Mrs. Hall if she was the sort to crumple at a few harsh words. Trust me, Mr. Charingford; I am quite able to judge what each can bear."

This was met with silence. Lydia felt herself frowning. Since when had Grantham thought her strong? Since when had he thought of her at all, except to label her a fribble?

Since he made a wager with a kiss for the stakes. Her hands tingled; Lydia shook her head, trying to drive that feeling away.

"You see that, do you?" her father finally said. "I don't think many men would. Still, be good to my daughter, Grantham, or you'll answer to me."

"Whatever you do could not be so harsh as what I would feel myself," he responded.

That was an even more puzzling answer, and she was pointedly *not* thinking of what it could mean when the door opened. Grantham stood a foot from her, his fingers wrapped around the handle of the door. His eyebrows rose at the sight of her.

"Miss Charingford," he said. "You're standing very close. Were you coming to get me?"

At his desk, her father shook his head. "She was listening at the door, Grantham," he said.

The doctor's eyebrows rose higher. "Miss Charingford," he said. "I didn't know that my conversation would be of interest to you."

"She always listens," her father said. He didn't smile as he spoke, but there was a touch of humor to his voice, a hint that he knew something of Lydia—and that he forgave her all her worst flaws.

"I always listen," Lydia said firmly. "You're no exception, so don't think you are. Doctor Grantham, if you're ready to go, I'm ready to get this finished."

"So," the doctor said, gesturing at the basket that Lydia carried. "What did you bring? Christmas puddings? Sweets for the children?"

There was a little smile on his face as he spoke, one that Lydia had no difficulty decoding. He imagined that she had no idea what it was like to live in poverty, that she had brought along the sort of insubstantial nothings that she might give to her young nephew.

"A few lengths of heavy, serviceable fabric," she replied. "A ham. Three pounds of flour, a pound of rice, some fruit, and several jellies." Her arm ached from the effort of holding it all.

He looked at her a little while longer before turning away. "That's not a poor choice."

"And yes," she said, staring at the side of his head, "I did bring a sack of horehound."

He smiled. "I knew it."

But before she'd outlined the contents of her basket, he'd thought she had brought nothing but sweets. He must truly think her an idiot, to bring nothing else for children who hadn't had a proper meal in months. She squared her jaw and walked on, refusing to look at him. It was always like this with him. He insinuated and implied, without actually coming right out and saying what he thought of her. Well, she'd foolishly agreed to this exercise, but that didn't mean she had to suffer his subtle insults throughout the whole process.

"Doctor Grantham, I wonder at your spending time with me if you find my personality so objectionable."

"On the contrary. I find your presence particularly invigorating."

Invigorating was one of those words like "interesting" and "nice." One used it to imply criticism.

"You think I'm naïve," she stated. The air was cold on her face.

He made a sound that came out as half-snort, half-chortle—a way of denigrating her without coming out and saying the words. Despite the chill in the air, Lydia felt her cheeks heat. Of all the men in the world, *he* was the last one she wanted laughing at her. This man knew her secrets. He looked at her too knowingly, judging her fall to an inch and holding her accountable in the dark recesses of his mind.

She glared at him hotly. "There is nothing wrong in thinking that children—any children—ought to have a treat at the holidays. The fact that they have so little means they are *more* deserving of a moment of enjoyment, not less. I'm sure horehound isn't practical in the sense of feeding the body, but it will feed the spirit and add to their joy. So don't you laugh at me for bringing it."

"Miss Charingford," he said in that sardonic voice of his, "I wouldn't dare laugh at you. Furthermore, I don't believe I did."

Oh, no. Not on the outside he hadn't. But inside... His eyes were dark and they sparkled with an unholy light, one that suggested he found her very amusing indeed. And that, in turn, sparked something deep inside her, something red and angry spreading over her vision.

"I am *not* naïve." She planted her feet and put down her basket.

He stopped and cocked his head at her.

"I know naïve," she told him. "Do you know what naïve is? Naïve is when, at fifteen, a man ten years your elder says he loves you, that he'll marry you as soon as you're old enough for your father to countenance the suit." She pointed a finger at him. "Naïve is when you love him back. Naïve is when you tell him that you're willing to do everything but that final act reserved for marriage—because you don't want to be stupid and become pregnant outside of wedlock."

One of his eyebrows rose, and she could almost hear him taunting her. *Didn't work out so well, did that?*

"Naïve is when he agrees, and you do everything but that one thing, that one thing that risks pregnancy, that one thing that you're saving for your wedding night. He tells you that he can't wait to do that one last thing." Her eyes smarted—just the cold of the wind; definitely not tears—but she lifted her gloves to her eyes and dashed away the liquid there. "He tells you how much more there is to do over and over as he rogers you senseless. I know what it means to be naïve. It's believing a man when he says this isn't how pregnancy occurs. Because you trust him, and nobody has ever told you what to expect."

His eyes had widened as she spoke. "Miss Charingford."

"Naïve is when he comes to dinner three months into your secret betrothal. You're wondering if tonight he'll tell your father." Lydia gritted her teeth. "I'll tell you when you *stop* being naïve, Doctor. It's when your father asks the man you believe to be your fiancé when he's bringing his wife up from town."

Doctor Grantham took a step toward her. "Oh, God."

"So don't tell me I'm naïve. Don't even think it." Lydia's voice had a quaver in it, and she hated that sign of weakness, that show of emotion over events that had come and gone. "After...after everything was over, after I realized how foolish I was, how ignorant I had been, I wanted to hate everything and everyone. But if I did, he would have won. He would have ruined me. I wasn't going to be a bit of rubbish just because he discarded me." She glared up at Grantham. "And I *refused* to break. I wouldn't do him the honor."

He was breathing almost as heavily as she was. His eyes burned into hers. His lips pressed together, and she could see that look on his face—that knowing, judging look. As if he needed *more* of a reason to look down on her.

That rush of heat passed, and Lydia felt almost unsteady on her feet. She took a deep breath, collecting her wits, and suddenly could not look at him at all. She'd just...she'd just...

Lydia put her hand to her forehead. "God," she said. "I don't know why I told you that."

"I do." He spoke slowly, hesitantly. "It's because you're angry, and you're kind. You can't be angry at the people who love you—your father, your mother. And you could never shout like that at the people who don't know what happened. That leaves me." He gave her a half-bow. "I know, although I should not. I'm the best target you have. I'm the only person you can scream at in all the world."

There was another sardonic half-smile at that.

"I'm not angry," she said in outrage. "I scarcely think of it after all this time."

"You're not angry?" He snorted. "I don't believe that for one instant, my dear. I'm not you, and *I'm* furious. If you told me his name, I would hunt him down and…"

"And what?"

He shrugged. "And I don't know. I was never the sort of boy to resort to fisticuffs as a child, and I haven't ended up that kind of man. But you can rest assured, my dear Miss Charingford, that nothing enrages me more than a man who lies to a woman about her own body." His lip curled.

Lydia bit her own lip. Doctor Jonas Grantham said a great many things to her, usually with that sardonic gleam in his eye. This was the first thing he'd said that she thought was entirely serious. His fingers clenched around the handles of his bag, and he looked off into the distance.

"What an odd thing to say." She picked up her basket. "I revealed so many things that might set you off—my foolishness, my misplaced trust, my failure to protect my virtue. And you are angrier that he lied to me than that he had intercourse with me?"

"Yes," he said savagely. "If I've learned anything, it's that we know next to nothing. Disease is a mystery. Health is inscrutable. The body itself is scarcely understood; we can only examine the secrets of the dead. And in all that dark ignorance, we're sometimes granted a rare moment of illumination, of understanding. The truth is a gift."

She felt quite peculiar. Her chest was too tight; her eyes stung. Lydia shook her head savagely; she didn't want to inspire that kind of vehemence.

Yet he made a short motion toward her, reaching out his hand before pulling it back. His jaw set, and he looked away.

"I believe," he said, "that there is a special place in hell for those who steal truth. And that man—whoever he is—I hope he is burning there."

Chapter Five

MRS. HALL WAS EIGHT MONTHS ALONG.

Jonas wasn't sure whether Miss Charingford would be taken aback by the other woman's very visible pregnancy or pleased by it—he never could guess how women would react.

But Lydia greeted Mrs. Hall as she greeted everyone—with a warm, happy smile, with bright conversation and compliments.

"I do love these curtains," Lydia said earnestly. "They are both functional and quite pretty. Never tell me you made them yourself?"

Jonas had never been able to manage that sort of small conversation. The labyrinthine rules attached to kind words usually left him bemused. And Miss Charingford was so *good* at it. He could have watched her make people smile for hours.

When he saw Mrs. Hall, he didn't see a woman who made curtains. She wasn't slender to his eye. She was undernourished. On her skinny frame, the pregnant bump of her belly sat like a grotesque lump.

There was a disease that was peculiar to women, and Mrs. Hall had it. It wasn't a disease that came from exposure to contagion. It didn't have a name. It was a sickness that took years to come on, and it crept up so gradually that people rarely noticed what was happening. It ravaged the rich and the poor alike—although, as with all illness, it landed most heavily on the poor.

Miss Charingford moved from Mrs. Hall to her children, never once looking at Jonas. She hadn't looked at him at all since her outburst.

Not that it mattered now; he had work to do. Jonas set about seeing to his patient.

"I lost another tooth," Mrs. Hall said quietly. "I lost it two nights ago."

Her skin was dry and scaly to the touch; she had dark bags under her eyes. Her children gathered around Lydia in a group. From Miss Charingford's basket, she'd taken a mass of wool stockings, which she distributed.

"Good of you, to bring her by," Mrs. Hall said. "Once was, I'd not take charity. Now…" She shrugged, as if to say she'd take anything she could get.

"Your heart rate is acceptable," he said, letting go of her wrist. "Just acceptable. There's a little fluid in your lungs. I think that so long as you have a chance to rest and recover, you should not suffer too much in the next month."

She nodded at this. "I've done eight already," she said. "I do know how it's done, Doctor."

"It is not the childbirth itself that worries me."

He didn't know the name of the disease she had, but he knew its symptoms. A man who wouldn't breed his mare two seasons in a row for fear of causing her an injury would be at his wife within weeks of childbirth. He'd plant his seed in a field that had not lain fallow for years, and like an overproduced field, the wife inevitably failed. Her back stooped. Her skin changed. Her eyes yellowed. Teeth fell out; bones that were once strong would snap at the smallest slip on icy pavement. Carrying a child was hard on a woman's body, and eight children, delivered ten months after one another, left a woman no room to recover.

Every time he tried to make the argument, though, he found that women disliked being compared to mares and fields, no matter how apt the analogy was.

As for the men—a fallow field, apparently, said nothing about a man's virility. But a wife who bore child after child formed a living, walking boast, one that he could parade in front of his compatriots. *Look at me! I'm a man!*

"The stuff that babes are made of comes from your own body, Mrs. Hall." He straightened and put away his stethoscope. "If the babe needs the material of bones, it comes from you. If it needs the material of skin, it comes from you. There's a reason you're losing your teeth, Mrs. Hall."

She looked away.

"You need to take a rest from bearing children. This babe likely won't kill you. The next one might."

Mrs. Hall glanced over at Lydia, now handing out oranges to the children. She lowered her voice. "And how am I to feed them all if I take a rest? I know they might not look like much to the likes of you, but they're precious to me." Her tone caught.

"How are you to feed them all if you perish?" he countered. "It is not a question of *if*, Mrs. Hall. It will happen. You're scarcely getting enough to eat. At some point, a child will come, and the act of producing it will exceed your strength. If you want to live, if you want to stay healthy for your little ones, you must stop bearing children."

Lydia could hear what he was saying, even though she didn't look in his direction. When Mrs. Hall had said that her children were precious to her, she'd smiled and looked down. But when Jonas spoke, her chin went up a few notches, and her grin turned into a show of teeth.

"What else am I to do?" Mrs. Hall said.

"No excuses," he said. "There is a way."

And he leaned in and told her.

"I DON'T THINK YOU'RE TRYING VERY HARD," Lydia said to Doctor Grantham as they left. "In fact, I don't think you're trying at all. She has a loving family and beautiful children. Did you notice that she had shoes for them *all?*" They'd been lined up in a row by the door, clean, if worn. "That takes a great deal of love. While I am sure that matters are difficult for her, with her husband deceased and her so recently pregnant..."

"Miss Charingford." Grantham was shaking his head and looking down, a little smile on his face. "Her husband passed away five years ago."

"Oh." She swallowed. "Dear. Will not the man who got her in that situation marry her, though?" She knew as she said it, though, that she'd just made herself look naïve again. Unmarried for five years? There must have been four children under that age in the house. If the man who was getting her with child hadn't married her yet, he was unlikely to do so now.

But Grantham didn't point out these obvious facts. He looked over at her and said, quite deliberately, "It's likely that she doesn't know who he is."

Lydia fell silent. That would imply that there were...a good number of men. "But she does honest work. She takes in laundry and mends and..."

"She doesn't walk the streets, if that's what you mean. And I have no doubt that with eight children, she is on her feet working as long as she can, as hard as she can, every day."

It made Lydia's back ache simply thinking about it. "I suppose," she finally said, "that she deserves...comfort, too. No matter what has happened to her."

Grantham gave a snort. "Comfort? Miss Charingford, you know precisely what is going on, even if you won't say it aloud."

Lydia felt her cheeks flush.

"Mrs. Hall is on her feet every minute she can work during the day, and when she can no longer stand, she works on her back. It's a common enough arrangement in tenement halls such as these. Likely she has ten or twelve men who visit her on a regular basis, who help to make up the difference in her expenses. The men can't afford a wife and a family; she can't afford not to have a husband."

Lydia was silent a moment longer. She thought of those shoes lined up, the curtains in the window. The note in the woman's voice as she said her children were precious to her.

Lydia now knew precisely how she valued them.

She thought of Grantham, leaning in at the end of the visit and whispering, and she felt a hot curl of anger.

"When you whispered to her, were you warning her of the danger of moral decay?"

She could still remember Parwine's gaze on her as he predicted damnation and death.

But Doctor Grantham simply rolled his eyes. "Tell me, Miss Charingford. Do I look like a rector?"

She glanced at him. The rector had floppy sideburns and always smelled of cabbage. Grantham's collar was white underneath a black cravat, but there the resemblance ended. He wore dark brown, which set off the dark color of his eyes. He was clean shaven, and he smelled faintly of bay rum. He looked... Very well, he looked handsome. Not that she cared about that.

She looked away and didn't answer.

"I'm a doctor; it is not my job to look to anyone's soul, but to see to their physical wellbeing. I told her that she should be using a French letter or one of the new capotes made from vulcanized rubber. Failing that, I suggested that she consider being fitted with a Dutch cap. The expense would be considerable for her, but not compared with the cost of a child."

Lydia turned to stare at him. "What are those things?"

"Prophylactics."

He tilted his head to look at her and must have seen the puzzled look on her face.

"For the prevention of pregnancy and, in the case of the former two, social disease," he spelled out. "The French letter goes over a man's penis and prevents the transmission of sperm; the Dutch cap over a woman's cervix. Neither is perfect, but they're certainly better than nothing."

The images that brought to mind... Lydia could scarcely breathe, imagining a sheath of rubber being fitted over a man's... Her cheeks flamed. "I am certain that this is not a proper subject of conversation between an unmarried lady and a gentleman."

He rolled his eyes again. "Tell me, Miss Charingford. Do I look like an etiquette advisor?"

"Not in the slightest."

"I'm not a virgin. Neither are you. And even if you were, there's no need for either of us to be missish about the matter. If a woman is old enough to push a ten-pound child through her birth canal, she can hear words like 'penis' and 'cervix.' These are medical terms, Miss Charingford, not obscenities."

He spoke in such a straightforward way, as if the penis and the cervix were parts of the body no more objectionable than fingers or toes, as if enrobing them in rubber were as simple as donning gloves. He didn't speak of what one would do after that particular glove were put on.

Lydia licked her lips and refused to look at him. "Have you used any of them?"

He didn't laugh at that highly improper question. "French letters, quite regularly. While I was in medical school, I had an arrangement with a widow who missed sexual intercourse, but didn't want a husband."

She couldn't believe that she'd asked. She couldn't believe that he'd answered. She really didn't want to think about the fact that Doctor Grantham was male, in possession of the standard male parts. That made her feel odd inside. Odd, and aware of her own body in a way that made her uncomfortable.

"French letters dull the sensation somewhat," he said. "If I were married, I'd ask my wife if she would consider being fitted for a Dutch cap. But that won't prevent social diseases like gonorrhea and syphilis." He looked at her directly, as if daring her to become flustered at the words he used.

"I really…" The protest seemed a formality, something she had to say. "I don't think that I should be having this conversation with you."

She was certain she shouldn't be. He'd just told her about his illicit arrangement with a willing widow. Men didn't tell women these things. And yet he hadn't boasted about the conquest. He'd stated it as a fact, as if sexual intercourse was just another thing that people did, one that had medical implications.

She blinked and shook her head furiously.

But his jaw had squared, and he turned to her. "When should I have this conversation with you, Miss Charingford? Do I wait until you're married and your body is already falling apart with the strain of carrying your seventh child in as many years? Should I wait until a fifteen-year-old girl catches pregnant because she was seduced by an older man?"

She couldn't breathe. "Don't, Grantham. Don't you dare talk about that."

"Why, because you might get angry again?" He set his bag down and turned to her deliberately. "I would rather infuriate you by telling you that sperm causes pregnancy and that there are methods to help prevent its transmission. The truth is a *gift*, Miss Charingford, and this conversation is a damn sight better than telling you you're going to die as a slut, and then poisoning you in hopes that you lose the babe."

He *was* furious, so furious that it took her a moment to comprehend what he'd said.

"Poisoning me?" she echoed.

"I told you earlier I thought you were angry with me. You should be angry. I could never tell if Parwine prescribed that remedy because he was ignorant, because he was trying to induce a miscarriage, or because he wanted you dead."

She couldn't breathe. She couldn't think at all. "I told you. I don't want to talk of that. I wish you'd forget it. I have."

"Tell me, Miss Charingford, before you miscarried, did you feel confused and faint? Were you dizzy? Was your skin more flushed than it usually was?"

"How did you know?" she breathed. "How did you know I miscarried?"

"A good guess. Prussic acid is also known as hydrogen cyanide, and it is one of the deadliest poisons known to man. Of course, the difference between a poison and a cure is the dose, but... At the level Parwine suggested? It wasn't a cure."

Lydia stared straight ahead, her eyes feeling dry as a desert. Her whole body seemed in agony remembering those cramps that had come. She shook her head, but the denial didn't help.

"So, no," he continued, "I won't forget that day. I held my tongue because Parwine was older and he knew better. I held my tongue because he had told me to keep quiet, and I thought that agreement more important than your wellbeing. And I have regretted it. I regretted it every day of my medical training. I regret it every day that I practice. I regret it now more deeply than you could imagine. I should have spoken at the time, and to hell with what Parwine told me beforehand. It shouldn't have mattered that he was the elder, and I was the young pup following him about. I wanted to be a doctor. The rule is that I should do no harm, not that I should do what is considered proper."

She'd never seen him so animated. She'd never felt so closed down, as if he'd stolen all the life from her. As if he were a repository for every dark emotion that she'd felt and shoved aside.

"So if you'd like to know, Miss Charingford, why I speak of penises and cervixes, I lay the blame at your door. There is no way I can apologize for what I could have prevented with a little plain speaking. All I can hope is that I will never make the same mistake again. I would rather open my mouth and say what is true than shut it for the sake of propriety. You claim you're not angry with me, Miss Charingford, but you should be. You should be."

She didn't feel anything at all. She wouldn't. She refused to let anger take root.

"You...you didn't agree with Parwine?"

"Not in the slightest particular. And for the record, Miss Charingford, when first I approached you last year... I had no idea who you were until you told me. I simply thought you were a reasonably attractive young lady. When I figured out who you were, I realized you were one of the bravest."

"But you are always so rude to me. So...so..."

He shrugged. "Miss Charingford," he said, "you may have noticed that I have a small number of defects in my character. I will tell you when I believe you are being missish—or silly—or overly cheerful, and yes, I make no attempt to cover my opinions in a coat of white sugar. But I have long believed that underneath that lovely, overly cheerful façade, you are actually a worthwhile individual."

He was looking at her in that way he had, the one that made her fingers curl. *Worthwhile* wasn't much of a compliment, but it was still too much. "I'm also the eleventh prettiest young lady in all of Leicester." She threw it out to remind herself how little she meant.

His cheeks actually colored at that—she had thought him utterly impervious to embarrassment—and he looked away. "As I said," he muttered. "You have good reason to be angry at me."

She couldn't think about what he'd said—none of it. He had to hate her. He *had* to think what Parwine did. He couldn't think well of her, because if he did...

It felt as if he'd just poked a raw, weeping wound—and she refused to be hurt. It *wouldn't* hurt. It wouldn't.

She gritted her teeth and swung her empty basket and thought of good things—of ginger cake baking in the kitchen, filling her home with the scent of spice and sugar, of boughs cut and laid on the hearth. She filled her mind with all the best of the holiday season, pushing away those old memories that flickered at the edge of remembrance—that one Christmas where there'd been no good cheer at all.

Just cramps and lies and...and hydrogen cyanide. She flinched from the thought.

"On the first day of Christmas," she sang, "my true love gave to me..."

He didn't join in. But as she sang to cut off all further discussion, all need for her to think on what he'd said, she could hear him laughing at her. Not literally, of course. But he knew.

He knew that she was pushing him away, silencing every conversation they might have had. He knew that she was slamming the shutters on her own dark storm of pain. He *knew*, and she didn't like it.

It was a long song, and she sang it slowly.

He only interrupted when she'd come near the end.

"Who wants lords a-leaping?" he asked. "If my true love brings me any number of lords shambling about in their cups on Christmas, I'll have words for her. Someone's going to break a bottle and cut his hand, leaping about like that, and then guess who's going to be roused from his warm home on the holidays to stitch him up? 'Oh, Doctor Grantham, you'd best come quickly!'" He made a rude noise.

Lydia simply looked at him. But she was grateful for that hint of levity, that retreat from the intensity that had come before. When she continued on with the song, her true love brought her lords a-leaping on the eleventh and twelfth days of Christmas, too.

When they arrived at her house, a boy stood from the step. He looked about six years of age—far too young to be out in the cold—but he seemed to vibrate with an urgency that emphasized the tear tracks on his face.

"Peter Westing," Doctor Grantham said. "What are you doing here?"

"It's about my brother."

"Good God. Has something happened to Henry?"

"The boiler collapsed," the young boy said, "and there was a slide of rubbish at the house."

Lydia could not visualize what it meant for a boiler to collapse—how on earth could metal *collapse?*—or for there to be a slide of rubbish inside a house. Grantham however, apparently could, because he grimaced at those words.

"He can't walk, Doctor, and he might get sacked." The little boy burst into tears on the last phrase, as if being sacked was a more dire consequence than the loss of mobility.

Doctor Grantham stood in place, staring straight in front of him. He shut his eyes. "Ah, God. Is he bleeding?"

"No."

"Can he move his toes? His arms?"

"Uh—yes, I think. But his leg is crooked, and he's in terrible pain."

"Thank God that is all that happened, then." He turned to Lydia. "Assuming Henry consents, Miss Charingford, I'll take you to see him tomorrow. You're going to see a twelve-year-old child who has broken his leg because his employer cannot clean his house." There was a note of bitterness in his voice. "And when he has been incapacitated, apparently his employer feels no compunction in letting him ago. After all, he had the temerity to trigger slides of rubbish. I dare you to find something good in that."

He set his bag on the stoop, undid the clasp, and peered inside. "Peter, I'll have to stop at home to get a few things if I'm going to be setting a fracture, but we'll be there as soon as we can."

"Yes, sir."

But instead of setting off immediately, he paused. "Miss Charingford." The words seemed unwillingly wrested from his chest.

"Yes?"

"You are only the eleventh prettiest woman in all of Leicester until you open your mouth."

Her mouth dropped open. To insult her, atop all the other horrible, awful, impolite, unacceptable things that he'd said? "Thank you so much for those kind words, Grantham," she snapped out. "I'm glad to know that my mannerisms so sink me."

But this time, he didn't smile at her; his eyes didn't sparkle with that familiar mischief. "Once you speak," he said, "you have no equal."

He turned away while her eyes were still widening in surprise. She found herself frozen in place.

Her body seemed unfamiliar to her, filled with aches and pains on the one hand, and on the other… A spark. One that sizzled through her. Lydia swallowed and shook her head, but she couldn't drive that feeling away.

He hefted his bag, flexed his free hand—he wasn't wearing gloves, which made absolutely no sense, as it was bitterly cold—and walked off, young Peter Westing trotting at his side. He walked quickly, and when he got to the corner, he didn't look back.

He didn't need to. She was still standing in place watching him go.

Chapter Six

IT WAS ALMOST SEVEN IN THE EVENING by the time Jonas found himself at his father's house. His arms ached—setting bones was tiring work, and Henry's break had been particularly tricky. But that was nothing in comparison with the weariness he felt in his soul.

No servant answered the door, of course; Henry had been the only one his father had allowed. These upcoming nights were the longest ones of the year. The sun set early. At this point, the house was pitch black. Jonas couldn't even see the gap in the rubbish as the door squeaked open. He found his way through the wreckage by feel. Toward the back of the room, he actually had to scramble over the piled-up detritus.

All this would have to be put in some semblance of order. But...not tonight. Not without daylight.

Jonas shook his head and found a candle on the hob and managed to light it. That scant wash of light—shifting over a wasteland of discarded metal—only made him shake his head in dismay. Nothing to do but wash his hands and prepare his father's dinner.

He still hadn't figured out what to say—what to do—by the time he ascended the stairs. He'd had a dozen conversations with his father in his mind already, and none had ended particularly well. But even those didn't prepare him for what he saw coming up the staircase. His father was seated on his bed, his arms crossed, and he glared in Jonas's direction.

"You're late," was what he said.

"Forgive me." The words came out sarcastic and hard. "I was unavoidably detained, treating the injury caused by your carelessness."

"*My* carelessness! If Henry had not been so clumsy—"

Jonas set the tray down in front of his father. "Do not talk of Henry to me at this moment. What am I to do with you? I can't ask anyone else to come into this house to look after you. It is downright hazardous."

"Hazardous? To those who are unable to walk in a straight line, perhaps, but—"

"I would call it a pigsty, but the greatest danger a sty presents is the possibility of mud. This place is a death trap, and I should have done something about it sooner. The only way you could make it more of a menace is if you installed spring-guns and man-traps."

Lucas Grantham squared his shoulders as best he could. "*You* should have done something?" he echoed, his voice arctic. "It is *my* home, *my* responsibility. Did I raise you to talk to me in that tone of voice? Tell me, did I?"

Jonas set a bowl of soup and a piece of bread in front of his father. "You didn't raise me to mince words in the face of stupidity."

"I raised you to respect your elders," his father spat. "To respect their wisdom and experience. To treat them with the courtesy that they deserve."

He had. His father had taught him to respect the old. If Jonas did that, though, he'd be prescribing prussic acid and traipsing merrily from autopsy to examination of infants. The elderly were as much a repository of hoary myths as they were keepers of wisdom. They'd just learned to voice their superstitions with greater authority.

And what did respect for his father even mean under these circumstances? Did it mean doing as he was told, keeping his mouth shut and his hands behind his back, no matter what the consequences?

"You also taught me to do what I believe to be right." He laid out a spoon. "I'm having a crew in tomorrow," he bit out. "And they are going to clean this place out."

His father almost choked. "I'll—I'll have the constable in again, I will. Thief—that's what you are, no better than a thief!" His face turned florid and blotchy, and he raised a fist in the air, shaking it. "You just want me to be dependent on you, to have nothing of my own. What kind of son are you?"

"Calm yourself." Jonas took hold of his father's wrist in some alarm. The pulse was hard and irregular, racing at a worrisome rate. He'd had one heart attack once, and that had left him in his current weakened condition. Another one...

"Calm myself! How can I calm myself when my only son is threatening to remove my livelihood?"

Once, Lucas Grantham would have shouted those words. Now, he could scarcely draw breath to speak them loudly. But his face reflected his fury, red and mottled.

He reacted this way any time Jonas suggested taking anything away. It was beyond rational explanation. He'd simply become fixed upon his scrap metal. The person he had been in his life was still there, but he'd hardened and solidified around this irrational core. Even if Jonas did hire a work crew—even if the constables allowed it to happen—he suspected that his father would work himself into an injury just watching. How could he do that to him?

But the alternatives—to let it go undone, or worse, to rob his father of all his dignity and to actually etherize him, as if cleaning his house were an act of mental surgery—were equally unpalatable. There was no good way out of this situation.

"No, no," he said soothingly. "You misunderstand me. I won't be removing anything from the premises." It wasn't lying, what he said. Just a change of mind, a change of tactics. "I just…"

He sighed, and thought of Lydia. He wasn't sure how his project was going. She'd talked to him today. He didn't think he'd shocked her too badly.

"There is a young lady I would like to bring to see you," he finally said. "Her name is Miss Lydia Charingford, and she is very dear to me."

His father lowered his fist. His breathing slowed. "A young lady?" he echoed. "That's good, Jonas. Is she pretty?"

"Very pretty."

Pretty didn't even begin to describe Lydia.

"I want you to meet her. All I want is to have some people in, to…rearrange things." He winced at the thought. "To put some of the loose items up in boxes. You know ladies these days, Father, with their wide skirts. After Henry's accident, I'd hate for anything to happen to her if she should brush up against the wrong pile."

"Just rearranging?" his father said in a querulous voice. "Not…not getting rid of anything, are they?"

"Just rearranging. I promise. Perhaps some of the boxes might be put out back, to make a little room. And then we can find someone to come in and do for you until Henry is on his feet again."

His father's pulse had returned to normal. His skin was no longer so dangerously flushed. For now, the crisis had been averted. He picked up his spoon and took a bite of soup. "That's good," he said. "So tell me about your Miss Charingford. How did you meet?"

LYDIA SPENT THAT NIGHT IN A DAZE. She scarcely heard her father and mother speak over dinner. She returned her mother's queries as to Mrs. Hall's health with a minimum number of words—there were children; Lydia had given them oranges—and tried not to think about all the things that Doctor Grantham had said.

She was not successful. Men and women couldn't talk of intercourse like that. If they could, it meant that all the pain she'd suffered out of ignorance had been heartbreakingly preventable. She couldn't think that.

And angry at him about what had happened? She wasn't *angry* at him. What a ridiculous idea. She didn't care about him, not one iota.

She thought that as she sat with her mother after dinner, embroidering. She often sat with her mother of an evening; on nights when he had nothing else to do, her father would join them. Tonight, however, it was just her and her mother, sitting together in companionable silence.

She didn't care about Grantham. Maybe, every time she saw him, he made her want to look away. But it had nothing to do with what Tom Paggett had done to her all those years ago. It was simply that she disliked his insincere smile, his knowing eyes. His gaze followed her across the room and she could feel it against her skin. He made her belly feel uncertain and fluttery, and she hated that mix of fear and anticipation, that moment where she couldn't tell if she wanted him to look at her more or never look again.

He made her *feel* naïve—like she had been back in that horrible time when Tom had made a fool of her.

No, she wasn't angry at him.

But you should be.

No. She couldn't think of what he'd said next, or she'd think of all the other things he'd told her.

Prussic acid is also known as hydrogen cyanide, and it is one of the deadliest poisons known to man.

She refused to accept that. She had to believe that horrible Christmas Eve was happenstance. She stabbed her needle blindly into the tablecloth she was embroidering. The alternative was too awful to contemplate. She'd been so confused, scarcely able to breathe. Halfway through December, the babe had stopped moving. She'd begun to worry. And then those cramps had come.

She stood and put her hands over her abdomen. "Mother," she said, "I'm not feeling well. If you'll let me retire early."

"Of course." Her mother frowned in worry. "Do you want me to send anything up for you?"

Lydia shook her head and climbed the stairs to her room.

It couldn't be true. None of it could be true. This was some sort of scheme on Grantham's part. She wasn't angry. She couldn't be. Why, she didn't feel a thing. Not one single thing. And what he'd said there at the end—

Once you speak, you have no equal.

It had made her breath catch and her pulse race, reminding her of the worst days with Tom. Back then, she'd hung on his every word, pretending to perfect propriety while others were around. She'd been eager to have him alone again so that he would say those things again and again. He'd made her feel as if he put the sun and the moon in the skies for her sake alone.

Lydia, darling, he'd moaned as he took her, *Lydia darling, I can't wait to make you mine.*

Lies. All lies. Doctor Grantham would know the medical term for the foolishness that made a woman want to believe a man when all evidence pointed to his insincerity, but Lydia knew what it felt like. It felt like stupidity. It felt like cramps. It was the absolute worst feeling in the world, the feeling of absolute betrayal as you sat at table in shocked silence. She knew what it felt like, and it was never, ever going to happen to her again.

Once you speak, you have no equal. She could hear his words in her head. She must have imagined that look in his eyes, that quiet strength in his voice. There must have been a hint of sarcastic inflection in his voice, a roll of his eyes that she had missed. He meant it sarcastically.

He had to have meant it that way, or those sparks that built up in her belly would burst into flame, and she was never burning again. Not for any man, no matter what he said.

She got into bed and pulled her pillow over her head.

No. She didn't think anything at all about Jonas Grantham. And she was absolutely *not* angry at him.

Chapter Seven

SHE WAS *DEFINITELY* ANGRY AT HIM, Jonas thought, as Lydia Charingford trooped beside him on the way to see Henry. She had thrust her fists into a muff and refused to meet his eyes. His attempts at conversation had been met with sniffs and a cold rebuff. They'd traveled halfway down Fosse Road, and she'd scarcely said a word.

By the time the park came into view, he was beginning to lose patience. He tried again. "Miss Charingford, might I carry your basket?"

"Was that a social grace on your part?" She stared straight ahead of her. "Doctor Grantham, I am positively amazed. Eventually, you may become fit to be let out in proper company."

"Only selfishness, my dear Miss Charingford." He let out an inward sigh. "When you swing it that way, you keep hitting the back of my leg."

"Oh." She didn't say anything else, but she did stop swinging the basket.

Henry did not live far from his father's house. One had only to cut across the park and walk down a few streets. But that brought Jonas down the dirt path toward the stage on which stood that massive edifice of a tree. It hadn't been decorated yet, and its branches gleamed like green poison in the midday sun.

Somehow, he'd thought this would be…well, definitely not *easy*. But he'd hoped it would be at least possible. He'd imagined that he would spend time in Lydia's company. She was always beyond fair-minded with everyone other than him.

A friend had once told him that he was like bitter coffee—positively habit-forming, once one acquired a taste for the beverage, but off-putting on the first few sips. So he'd harbored no illusions that she would love him instantly. But she might have moved from hatred to approbation, and from there, he'd hoped that she wouldn't grimace too much at the thought of him.

Now, anything other than the dislike she heaped on his head seemed inconceivable.

"So," he tried again as they approached the tree, "your father read me another lecture today when I came by for you. If he thinks so ill of me, I'm surprised that he lets you out at all."

Little spots of pink blossomed on her cheek. "Don't you talk about my father," she said in a low voice. "And how dare you imply that about me?

There's nothing objectionable in walking in public with a man, even if he insists that he's a doctor and not a gentleman."

He looked up to the sky, which answered only with clouds. "I only said—"

"I know perfectly well what you meant, Doctor Grantham. You think that after my indiscretion, he should have locked me away, never allowing me to be in the company of another man."

"I do *not* think that." He bit out those words. "I have never said that. I never will."

She wouldn't look him in the eyes.

"It would make no sense to think that, as I enjoy being in your company."

"Stop," she said, shaking her head. "Please stop."

So Jonas did. He stopped walking in front of the stage, the dark green branches of the tree looming over him like a menacing creature made of holiday cheer.

"Listen to me, Lydia," he snapped. "If you're going to despise me, do me the favor of hating me for the things I've said, rather than the ones you've imagined."

"I'm imagining things?" A wild light came into her eyes. "You think I'm imagining that you look at me like I'm a mistake that should have been put away? You think I'm imagining the way you weigh me on your scale of moral superiority and find me lacking? I know precisely what you think of me."

He actually heard himself growl at her. "I don't have a scale of moral superiority. You know this is all balderdash. You can tell yourself that I'm thinking myself superior to you all you like, but it has no relation to the truth. You see the good in all the world—all the world, Lydia, except me. Why do you think that is?"

"Because you—"

"You don't want to know what I really think of you. It's easier for you to set me up as a whipping boy for all your aggressions—"

She made an outraged sound and swung the basket she carried at his black bag. She aimed it at him as if she were a fencer, and their respective bags their swords. He was so surprised that he scarcely had time to step out of the way.

"Careful!"

"Go ahead. Tell me it isn't ladylike to resort to violence. Tell me that it confirms what you believe of me—that I'm impulsive, hotheaded, and foolish."

"Hit my person all you want," he replied, "but by God, Lydia, if you jostle my bag, you could break the bottle of laudanum. It will get all over my stethoscope, and I will be up all night cleaning it. Do you have any idea how many little parts and tubes there are to a binaural stethoscope?"

Not to mention the mess it would make of his record book. That was three months of visits, symptoms carefully recorded and pored over of an evening, trying to ferret out cause and effect. Plus, the bag had impossible-to-clean corners and seams. It would be sticky for *months* afterward.

He shuddered and set his bag carefully on the stage. "Punch me, but leave my medicine out of it."

"I'm not going to strike you in public," she said scornfully.

He jumped up on the stage, and then, before she could protest, hauled her up to stand beside him. The tree was fat and tall, but there were a few feet of space behind it, shielded from public view by the needled branches.

He held up his hands, palms facing toward her. "Go ahead," he said, and this time, he let a note of mocking infect his tone. "Hit me. Or do you think you're too weak to cause damage?"

She balled her fist and hit his hand. The shock of the strike traveled up his arm, clear to his elbow. She packed a surprising power for her size, along with better follow-through than he'd expected.

While he was still blinking in surprise, she hit his other hand, her teeth clenched. "God damn you, Doctor Grantham."

"He probably will." He was doing it right now, presenting her before him, her hair slipping from her coiffure, those curls dangling at her cheeks, asking to be brushed away.

She swung at him again, a little more wildly. "I hate you."

"I'm sure you do."

She glared at him. "I am not—I repeat—I am *absolutely not*—angry at you." This was punctuated by another blow. If she'd actually been trying to hurt him, he suspected he'd be in pain. But she concentrated on his hands, striking them with all the force of her fury.

The scent of pine surrounded them; branches tickled his lower back. She shifted her stance, and the tree vibrated as her skirts brushed its needles.

"Far be it from me to contradict you, but you appear to be quite angry with me."

She looked up into his eyes. "I can't be angry with you," she snarled. "You haven't done anything wrong, and if I were angry with you, it would be *irrational.*"

"Not irrational. Just not very fair."

"If I were angry, it would mean that I still hurt, that I still cared about what happened to me. It would mean that I hadn't put it all behind me. And I have."

Her eyes dropped and she looked at her fists, as if just realizing that she had been hitting him. Her hands flexed. Her face turned up to his, stricken, as she recalled what she had just said. "I have," she repeated. "I don't think about it all."

He couldn't say anything.

"Do you know what I hate most about your eyes?" Her voice had fallen to a whisper, and he couldn't make himself look away. "When I look into them," she said, "I see my own reflection in them. Mirroring back all the things—" She choked.

Her skin turned white. That meant the capillaries in her skin were constricting. He could almost have guessed her pulse from the labor of her breath. She'd be feeling cold and light-headed right about now.

"Breathe deeply," he suggested.

She didn't. Instead, she doubled over, as if she were the one who had been struck. She held her stomach.

"Oh, God," she whispered. "I haven't put it behind me."

He stepped closer to her. She made a sharp, keening sound, wind whistling between her teeth. She wrapped her arms around herself. He wanted to touch her, to lay a hand on her shoulder. But just as he was on the verge of reaching out, she straightened and looked in his eyes.

"I am angry." She said those words carefully, trying them on as she might put on a hat in a shop. She must have found the fit to be superior, because she gave a little nod. "I'm furious. Absolutely furious. I could *kill* Tom Paggett, if he were here."

Tom Paggett. Jonas made a mental note of the name. He was already wondering what to do about the man, when Lydia burst into tears.

It was absolutely the last thing he'd expected. She didn't cry daintily. She stood in place, fumbling in her skirts for a handkerchief. And finally, Jonas let himself move. He took those final steps toward her and did what he'd longed to do for so many months.

He put his arms around her. And to his utmost relief, she not only let him, she curled her hands around him and pulled him closer.

For that moment, he could let himself glory in the feel of her—the sweet softness of her, the feel of her warmth against his body. He could simply hold her and pray.

He could almost have cried alongside her.

Those gut-wrenching sobs—even if he'd cared nothing at all for her, they'd have tugged at his heartstrings.

"Shh," he whispered. "Shh. I'm sorry."

He knew she didn't care who he was—that she was too anguished in that moment to do anything but weep, and take what little comfort he could give. He was nothing more than a shoulder to her.

Still, he was glad that it was his arms enfolding her, that his lapels took the brunt of her grief. He was the one who stood there as she wept, the one who felt when those shudders began to subside. Each minute that passed seemed precious. When the sobs faded to sniffles, he wiped her eyes with his handkerchief.

"I don't know why you're doing this," she sniffed as he dabbed at her cheeks. "You're being kind, but you always make fun of me."

He ran his hand down her shoulder. "I never make fun of you."

"You say such horrid things about me."

"I never say horrid things about you," he contradicted. "I tell you exactly what I think of you, and you never believe me."

"You're sarcastic and contradictory."

He sighed and breathed in the smell of her, sweet and uncomplicated. "Well, yes. That, I must admit to. But half the things I say to you in sarcasm, Lydia, I really mean. I just can't bear to leave them unsaid."

"But if you don't think badly of me..."

He didn't answer. He wanted her to lift her head at this moment. He wanted her to look him in the eyes and realize that he loved her. He wanted her to love him back. For now, he'd settle for this—for Lydia in his arms, Lydia finally talking to him like a man rather than a monster to be scorned. For once, the size of that dreadful Christmas tree seemed welcome, affording them this small amount of privacy. He could hold her, and nobody would see.

"You told me," she said accusingly into his chest, "that I was welcome in your bed."

He looked up at the top of the tree. For a brief moment, he contemplated giving her a polite response. But... No use pretending he was anyone other than who he said. "You are," he said quietly. "Any man who says otherwise is probably not being truthful. And my faults usually run to too much truth, rather than too little."

She sighed; he could feel her chest move against his. Lovely feeling, that.

"I only mind a little bit," he said. "As I said before, I wonder sometimes how you can have a kind word for any man at all. You've singled me out. I'd rather be special in some way than no way at all."

"That's ridiculous," she said.

"I know."

She hid her face against his shoulder. He'd never noticed before how much a breath could say. It seemed more than the transportation of air to lungs. The act of breathing with another person—of accepting silence together, of simply *living* in tune with the rhythm of someone else's existence—was deeply intimate. They said more to each other with quiet respiration than they'd managed in sixteen months of bickering.

Lydia spoke first. "I think, Doctor Grantham, that I've been unfair to you."

He shut his eyes. It wasn't love, but by God, he'd take it. It was hope, one little ray of hope, that there was a chance for him. That she might know the worst of him and want him anyway. And she didn't let go of him. He liked the feel of her against him. She was warm and sized right for his arms.

"You didn't do anything wrong," she finally said. "You were—how old when you accompanied Parwine? No older than I am now. You were there to learn, not to speak. I should never have blamed you."

He let out a breath.

"There." She gave a little hiccough, and then, of all things, a smile touched her face. "Now you can't say that I never have a kind word for you. Did you really say back there that you would rather I hit you than disturb the cleanliness of your bag?"

He couldn't help but smile back. "I did. And it's true. I'm a horribly flawed man, Lydia."

Another long moment. She rested her cheek against his shoulder, and for those moments the world was perfect.

"I have never given you leave to use my Christian name," she pointed out.

"Yes, you have," he responded. "I'm no expert in these matters, but when a lady cries on my shoulder, I take it as tacit permission to address her by name."

"Hmm," she said, but didn't disagree.

Holding her in his arms was having its inevitable effect. He shifted against her. "Little as I wish to suggest we end this embrace…it would probably be a good idea."

"Would it?"

Jonas paused, this time a little longer. He wasn't going to say it. He really wasn't going to say it. He was… Oh, hell. He *was* going to say it.

"It has been eighteen months since I last had occasion to make use of a French letter, and I am becoming physically aroused. It will become apparent in a minute or so, and that will prove embarrassing."

Lydia gasped against his chest. "My God. Are you always this plainspoken?"

"It's a natural physiological reaction," he returned.

She pulled away, but just enough that she could look into his face. "Doctor Grantham, never tell me that you're ashamed of a natural physiological reaction."

She hadn't let go of him. She hadn't let go. Hope was not just present, it was incandescent. He found himself smiling down into her face. "Yes, I am. I have not completely crushed the restrictions that social mores place on me, however absurd they are," he countered. His hand stroked her hair as he spoke. "I'm working on that."

"Then work on it for another two minutes," she said quietly. "I'm not done."

"Ah, Miss Charingford." That was all he said, but he put his arms around her, pulling her closer, breathing in her old hurts, and exhaling the emotions he had not yet managed to voice.

"The part that makes me angriest," she whispered into his chest, "is that I miss *this*. I miss being held. I miss the feel of lips on mine, of arms around me. I miss the feel of warmth. Sometimes, I even miss all those things that he did to me. It's a palpable hunger, one that eats me up inside. I shouldn't want that. There's something wrong with me."

Jonas cleared his throat. "Actually ..."

She made a little noise.

It wasn't as if he was suddenly going to fool her into believing him proper. "This is not my area of expertise, Miss Charingford, but there are specialists in London who do nothing but treat women who do not enjoy intercourse. It is physiologically normal to feel as you do."

His erection was becoming all too apparent. She had to have noticed by now. Even if there weren't that thick bar growing between his legs, pressing lightly against her body, there was the change in his breathing.

"Really?" she asked.

"Really."

He could detect the changes in her. He was standing too close to her, too attuned to her, to miss the signs. Those telltale capillaries in her skin widened, and her skin flushed pink with blood flow. Her lashes fluttered down; her mouth opened a little bit. She held him too tightly, too precisely.

"Sometimes," she said, "it feels like there are some hurts that can only be cured by this. By warmth. And touch."

He slipped two fingers over her wrist, taking her pulse. He knew all too well the difference between a resting heart rate and an aroused one, and that knowledge of her body's response only fed his own desire.

He bent over her a little more, his lips breathing warmth against her ear. Just a little kiss. He could give her a little kiss, now.

But he didn't. He knew all too well that physical arousal needn't mean that she liked him. She'd only just decided not to hate him. She'd needed a shoulder to weep on, a form to hit, a generic repository for all the emotions that she couldn't fit in her life. She didn't need a kiss from a specific man, no matter how much he specifically wanted to give her one.

"Miss Charingford," he said, "Henry awaits, and I shouldn't delay any longer. We must go on." He pulled away from her. She looked up at him, her eyebrows screwed up in quizzical confusion.

But when he offered her his arm, she took it. He set his fingers over her wrist and took comfort in the beat of her pulse—a little faster than could be explained by the mild exercise of walking.

Chapter Eight

JONAS HAD SET AND SPLINTED HENRY'S LEG LAST NIGHT. He'd given the boy a dose of ether when he'd set the leg, enough that he'd not been in his right mind by the time he left. Henry had waved him off, grinning goofily. It was his father who looked on grimly.

This morning, the drug had worn off. Henry was propped up in a chair with nothing to do but look out the window. His pupils had returned to normal size; his eyes were sunken and dark.

Lydia came forward and sat in a chair next to the boy. While Jonas checked his vital signs, she introduced herself.

"I am Miss Lydia Charingford," she said warmly. "Doctor Grantham asked me to come because he thought I needed to see an example of someone who conducts himself with decorum under difficult circumstances."

Henry—who had slouched every minute that Jonas had known him—straightened subtly. "He did?"

"He did," Lydia said, with absolutely no regard for the truth. "And I can see that he chose a good subject."

"Right." Henry nodded. "Speaking of difficult circumstances. Doctor, I don't suppose you could give me more of that…whatever it was you gave me last night, could you? My leg aches something awful."

"No," Jonas said. "I can't. I don't carry around ether as a general matter. And I prefer not to administer laudanum unless it's absolutely necessary. It contains morphia, which causes constipation and impotence."

"Uh." Henry glanced at Lydia, and his cheeks flushed. "Did you just say—uh—"

Jonas gave him a repressive look, and Henry bit his lip.

Lydia simply smiled angelically. "Someday, you'll thank him for it."

If anything, Henry turned pinker. "Don't need laudanum," he muttered. "Doesn't hurt that much, anyway. I'm practically healed already. I'll be walking in no time at all."

He probably thought that was true. And in a few days, the worst of the pain would fade. Last night, there'd not been much chance to explain matters.

Jonas sat down on a chair next to Lydia. "Henry," he said, "you fractured the lower end of your tibia right by your foot. If you walk on it before it is healed, you will displace the fracture, and any subsequent weight you place on it thereafter could very well make the fracture a compound one."

Henry frowned. "What does that mean?"

"If you walk on your leg, you might break it again in multiple spots. A compound fracture so close to your joint would likely mean amputation. You must not walk on it until it is healed."

Henry gave him a stoic nod. "How long's that going to be? Once it's stopped hurting?"

"You won't be able to move your leg for three weeks."

"Three weeks!" Henry's eyes widened. "Doctor Grantham, I can't go three weeks without pay."

"Henry," Jonas said, "not only are you not going to move for three weeks, after that you will wear a splint, and you will not put excessive weight on your limb."

Henry's jaw squared and he looked off into the distance. "Let's say one week without moving," he said sullenly. "And then—"

"This is not a negotiation, Henry. If you want to keep your leg, you must stay off it."

Henry didn't say anything, but his jaw set mulishly.

Beside him, Lydia leaned forward. "Surely something can be managed. Perhaps, as you were injured at work, your employer might be willing to pay something..."

"Ha." Henry stared down at the floor. "You haven't met the old—" He looked up at Jonas, and then looked away, remembering that his employer held a special position in Jonas's life. "You don't see it. I'm not clever, but Peter and Billy are. If I have no wages, my brothers will have to get work. And if they give up their places in the boys' school..." Henry poked morosely at the cast on his leg. "How long, do you think, before I can risk it? A week and a half, maybe?"

"I said you weren't allowed to move," Jonas told him. "I never said you couldn't work. As it happens, it's lucky for you that your injury is tricky. I'm writing a paper on recovery of the use of a limb after a difficult fracture, and I find myself in need of a subject. Someone who will do exactly as I say and nothing more. If you agree to allow me to write you up, I'll pay you for your time."

"I don't need your charity."

Jonas had found him the job with his father. He'd been the one who let matters slide, dithering about what needed to be done simply because it was his father. It wasn't *charity*, not in the slightest. It was blood money.

"You think I'm doing this for your benefit?" he snapped back. "You'd have to remain still all day—no running, no playing with the other boys until

I tell you you're able. Any man can stand about on his feet all day. But it takes real talent to remain sitting."

Henry frowned. "It does?"

"Yes. In fact, I'm not sure you can manage it. Sitting all day with nothing to do but twiddle your thumbs. And don't think I'll pay you if you can't comply with the stringent requirements I have."

Beside him Lydia twitched, leaning down to open her basket.

"Almost nothing to do," she said. "I've brought a bandalore. Shall I show you how to use it?"

"YOU'RE NOT EVEN TRYING TO WIN THIS WAGER," Lydia said, as they left the small house behind. "You can't very well bring me along on your house calls on the assurance that there is no bright side to be found, when you are planning to sweep in and hire the poor boy yourself."

He looked over at her and smiled, and that expression made her feel…

No, it didn't make her feel anything. She looked away.

"I don't even have to look for the bright side! I was prepared to talk about the way he cares for his brothers—anyone can see he loves them—but then you went and ruined things for yourself. You have already counteracted any repressive, morbid things you might say. Henry suffered a terrible accident, but by an act of generosity, he will do very well. Your actions make no sense."

He simply smiled. "On the contrary. I am doing precisely what I planned."

"Do you not want to win?"

"I want to win. I want to win very much." He'd offered her his arm again on the way back and she'd taken it. Some men folded a hand over a woman's when they walked with her. He set two fingers against her wrist, yet that lesser contact seemed intimate in a way that she couldn't explain.

She glanced down.

Or maybe she could explain why it seemed so different. He'd insinuated his hand in that small gap between her gloves and her cuff, and his fingers were bare. She could feel the warmth of his skin directly on hers.

"You are not wearing gloves," Lydia said in shock.

He simply tapped his fingers against her wrist and kept walking. "Very observant, Miss Charingford."

Little flakes of snow drifted down.

"Why are you not wearing gloves? Your hands must be almost frozen. It's extremely cold out."

But his fingers were warm, exceedingly warm.

"I never wear gloves when I pay house calls." His forefinger drew a little line down her wrist as he spoke. "In fact, I almost never wear gloves anymore."

He stared straight ahead of him as he spoke.

"I hesitate to ask...but is there some reason for this? You are not wealthy enough to be that eccentric."

A faint smile touched his lips. "Perhaps you may have noticed this, Miss Charingford," he said, "but I have a small number of defects in my character. This one stems from scientific ignorance."

"Now you have piqued my curiosity."

"There is a study by Doctor Semmelweis in Austria," he said. "He has been much maligned for it, but I see no fault with the methodology. Semmelweis worked in a hospital in Vienna, and he decided to make one tiny little change in his practice. After he performed an autopsy—and before he delivered a child—he washed his hands in a solution of chlorinated lime." He looked over at her. "He found that when he did so, the incidence of childbed fever was reduced by an astonishing ninety percent."

"Good heavens."

There was a sparkle to his eye, a liveliness in his step. His speech grew faster, more confident. "Think of that, in connection with John Snow's discovery. In the midst of a cholera epidemic, Snow removed one pump handle—and with that single action, stopped the spread of disease. Every few years brings a new medical discovery, a new way of looking at the world. There is more happening that we do not understand and cannot see. But those two things, taken together... If Semmelweis is right, doctors are conveying sickness. That makes us pump handles, bringing illness from patient to patient. I started washing my hands after seeing any patient who had a contagious disease."

"What a terrible thought."

"And then I would put my hands in my gloves, and I would start to wonder. What if I hadn't completely scrubbed the contagion away? If I had not, my gloves would be contaminated. I'd be walking around with my hands in mitts that were positively squirming with whatever it is that transmits disease." He looked away. "One mistake, and I might contaminate my gloves forever. Needless to say, I stopped wearing gloves."

He pursed his lips as he spoke.

"That is..."

He gave her a rueful look. "Odd? I've engaged in the most amazing screaming matches with other physicians over the practice. Doctors are gentlemen. Gentlemen have clean hands." He set his jaw. "Most of the young men my age agree, but the older ones... They've been going from autopsy to childbirth for years, and refuse to admit that they might be the source of contagion themselves. To be honest, I think that the medical profession will only fully institute the practice of hand-washing once our elders stop practicing."

"I wasn't going to say it was odd," said Lydia. "I actually think that is rather an extraordinary thing to do. I'm impressed."

He let out a laugh. "Trust you, Miss Charingford, to turn my world upside down. You take my most admirable characteristics and twist them into faults. But when I admit something that I am sure exposes me for the strange man that I am, I receive the first compliment that I have ever received from you."

"Surely not the first!"

"The absolute first. I've counted."

She swallowed. The way he was looking at her… She felt like a teapot set on the hob, warming to a slow boil under his gaze.

"There is something you said earlier that I don't understand," Lydia said.

"Miss Charingford." He folded his arms and looked at her forbiddingly. "I'm sure I said a great deal that you found unfamiliar." His mouth set in a straight line. "I suppose it's too much to hope that you have a question about gonorrhea. Those questions are so much easier to answer."

She paused and tilted her head. "I think," she said, "that you may have the most dreadful sense of humor of any man that I have ever encountered."

He didn't protest. "I'm fairly certain I do." He glanced down at her. "And yet you have not run screaming. I count that as progress; I have become positively acceptable. Now what was it you were going to ask?"

"I was going to ask about what you said earlier. That you'd…that you'd…not used a French letter in eighteen months." She swallowed. "I know I shouldn't talk about this, but…but you actually answer my questions. Tell me if this is too impertinent—"

"No such thing." But his voice had become even more forbidding.

Still, Lydia felt heartened. "It's acceptable for men to…to visit women without being married. Like with Mrs. Hall, the other day. Are you telling me you don't?"

"It has nothing to do with what is acceptable and what isn't. I don't wear gloves because I'm afraid that they might carry contagion. I'm not about to sheathe myself in a woman who could give me a disease. When I established myself here in Leicester, I determined that I wouldn't have intercourse at all until I married." There was a little smile on his face. "I didn't think it would take quite so long, or I'm not sure I would have made such a hasty vow."

"So you are looking for a wife? Good, God, Doctor Grantham. Sixteen months ago you reached girl number eleven in Leicester. What woman are you on now, number forty?"

"It…it hasn't been like that." He grimaced.

Lydia gave him her best wide-eyed innocent's look. "I realize the search will be difficult, but surely somewhere in the entirety of Leicester, there must be at least one female who is so undiscriminating that she is willing to accept even you."

"At least one?" He grinned broadly at her, understanding her teasing for what it was. "My. Praise like that will go straight to my head."

"Do take it to heart. Even someone like you should be able to find a wife."

"Thank you," he said. "Even someone like me appreciates the sentiment."

"Perhaps if you were a little less circumspect at displaying your income, you could convince number fifty."

He laughed out loud. "You viper," he said, but the words had no real heat to them. "It's those defects in my character again. If you must know, I'd make a devil of a husband—always being woken at half two in the morning to go see someone who's taken ill, telling my wife the truth no matter how inconvenient or unflattering it might be." He shook his head and smiled at her. "Caring more about neatness than my personal wellbeing. Making terrible jokes."

"You're not all that terrible."

"Thank you. I shall have that engraved on a plaque and presented to future candidates with your recommendation. The real problem is that I'm unfortunately constant in my affections. I've had my eye on one particular woman for more than a year. It wouldn't be fair to marry anyone else with my attention thus engaged."

"Oh, too bad," Lydia said, shaking her head. "And she is not undiscriminating?"

"Alas," he said, looking straight at her. "She is damnably clever, and I wouldn't wish her any other way."

The way he looked at her made her heart thump, her breath catch. For a second, those dark eyes seemed to have no end to them, as if she were looking into a hall of mirrors and seeing reflection upon reflection echoing into infinity.

For just one second, she felt a tug of yearning.

"I think," Lydia said slowly, "you might have to lower your sights."

"I've tried." He gave her a rueful grin. "God knows I have. But the view to the heights is so inspiring that every time I convince myself I must move on, I'm charmed anew."

It was almost impossible to conceive. For all his black humor, Doctor Grantham was attractive. Those velvety black eyes seemed to catch her in and pull her to him. He looked at her with a dangerous, wicked intensity. His lips were full and curled up in a smile. If he hadn't been so set on another woman, she might have found herself dangerously taken with him.

"What of you?" he said. "What's your excuse? Yes, yes, I know; you just threw Stevens over last month. But I would have thought that for the eleventh prettiest unmarried woman in all of Leicester, there would be a rush of men to take his place."

"Do be serious, Doctor Grantham, and think of what you know of me." Her voice lowered. "I did not become pregnant through immaculate conception. I had sexual intercourse. I am the farthest thing from a virgin."

He raised his eyebrow at her. "I'm a doctor, Miss Charingford, and even *I* can't always tell on close examination whether a woman is a virgin. Besides, the hymen is just a membrano-carneous structure situated at the entrance of the vagina. It is of substantially less physiological relevance to a man in the throes of passion than the vagina itself."

"Yes, but…" She sputtered. "It's not about the hymen itself, it's about—"

"As it is, *I've* had sexual intercourse. And even though it has been too damned long since the last time, I don't go about trumpeting the fact. You don't, either. This is an irrelevancy, Miss Charingford."

She simply sniffed in response to that. "You're being difficult. I'm fickle, and I have a temper. I not only cried off from my last fiancé, I threw him over by tossing two glasses of wine punch in his face at a dinner party."

"I wish I had been there to see it. Agreeing to marry Stevens, by the way, doesn't speak highly of your taste. He was a regular ass." He shrugged. "But that only confuses me further. Possessing poor taste in men doesn't hinder a woman in the getting of husbands. It generally helps."

"My God, you are obtuse." Lydia shook her head. "For a man as outspoken as you are, you are remarkably obtuse. I'm not so much of a catch."

"That is how you see yourself?"

"Oh, I forgot. I'm the eleventh prettiest girl in all of Leicester." Her chin raised a notch. "I suppose with that, I ought to be able to catch at least the twenty-second most desirable man—accounting for my perfidy and my tainted past."

"I have never said that. Surely, in all of Leicester—once we include the surrounding areas—somewhere there must be some man who is undiscriminating enough to marry you."

Lydia felt curiously light. "I'm sure there is," she said, very quietly. "And what I most fear is that I am undiscriminating enough to let him do it."

He didn't say anything to that.

"Take Captain Stevens, my former fiancé. Not only did he threaten my best friend, but he was putting the most extraordinary pressure my father. And I knew that when he asked. I agreed to marry him, because I thought if I did, it would stop. I convinced myself that we would do well together— that he cared for me, that he would make a good husband. I knew I didn't care for him in that way, and that was his greatest recommendation. I thought that made me safe."

Grantham didn't say anything to that.

"Listen to what I am saying. I convinced myself that George Stevens was safe when he was leaning on my father." Lydia threw her hands in the air. "And Tom Paggett—I wasn't the only girl he interfered with. A few months after he left town, the residents of his new city caught him with a thirteen-year-old child. They couldn't prove...in any event, he was only thrown in the stocks, but the people were so riled that they threw more than fruit, and he..." Lydia didn't want to finish the sentence, but she didn't need to. Grantham likely knew what happened to a man who was hit with stones at close range. "And so yes, Doctor, I'm sure that there is some man who will be sufficiently interested. But what I most fear is that I'll convince myself that he's safe. I'll marry him because it will make my family's life easier, and tell myself again and again that he's the best thing for me." Her jaw clenched. "All the while, he'll be nothing more than a common criminal. You were right about at least one thing. I am overly cheerful, and no group less deserves my cheer than the men who are interested in..."

She bit her lip. She couldn't say that word, not to a man. She *couldn't*. But he was looking at her, and somehow she found the courage.

"No group less deserves my cheer than the men who are interested in my vagina. But we were not talking about me. We were talking about you." She looked down. "Now that I've discovered that you aren't as bad as I thought, I'm amazed anew. How is it that you could have been fixed on one person for so long? I can understand her not returning your regard—that makes perfect sense."

"Of course," he said repressively.

"Not that I mean to be cruel, but you are a little..."

"I am well aware of my flaws," he said. "We can save their enumeration for some later time, if it pleases you."

"So—she has refused your suit. Unequivocally. And you are still fixed on her? That seems surprisingly illogical of you."

Grantham looked at her. "She has not refused my suit. If you must know, I haven't asked."

"Haven't asked her? Doctor Grantham, you can tell a patient straight out that she ought to make a rubber mold of her cervix. You cannot make me believe that you are unable to propose to a woman."

"The time has never seemed right." He folded his arms. "There were other people about, or she didn't seem to be in the proper mood, or I ruined everything by making a stupid joke about gonorrhea. I have not completely crushed my sense of social obligations. In any event, even I have fears. I am afraid that she will turn me down. And once she does so unequivocally, that will be the end of it all."

"Does she even *know* that you feel this way about her?"

"She knows," he said calmly. "At this point, she would have to be an idiot not to know, and she's not that. I suspect that for her own inscrutable reasons, she doesn't want to admit it to herself. I am ornery and difficult, but I am not a particularly subtle individual, and there can be no other explanation for my attention to her."

He looked into her eyes as she spoke, and she felt an unwelcome thrill deep in her belly, as if these words had found their target deep in her solar plexus. She shook off that odd feeling and turned away from the direct intensity of his gaze.

"Believe it or not, Doctor Grantham, I am beginning to like you. Your personality may be…well, a bit abrasive, but it grows on me. I want to help you, give you a push. Even abrasive, difficult men deserve happiness. I should be able to figure out who you're enamored of without too much difficulty."

"Yes, you should," he said.

Every sentence sent a little pulse of excitement through her.

She made herself look up at him with a smile on her face. "Maybe I could help you. Put in a good word for you, that sort of thing."

He smiled faintly. "When you figure it out," he said, "I'd be much obliged. Tell her that I may be difficult, but I am remarkably constant in my affections, that I have thought of her every day for these last sixteen months. Even when it made no sense."

And that left her with the biggest thrill of all, her whole body vibrating with an unexplainable urgency.

Chapter Nine

FOR THE SECOND NIGHT IN A ROW, Doctor Grantham had left Lydia in a state of bewilderment. After he'd returned her to her doorstep, her confusion had refused to untangle. She'd thought of what he'd said as she entered the house, throughout dinner. She was still thinking about it when she joined her parents in the back parlor.

He'd admitted that he'd been taken with a woman for more than a year. It was such a romantic thing to say. Which was why she could hardly countenance it from him.

If someone had asked her before today, she would have imagined that he was the sort to say that all women were alike. He'd use medical terms. One vagina, he might say, was much like another. Both provided the same stimulation to the pleasure centers. She bit her lip, imagining him saying that in his dark, gravelly voice.

But he hadn't said that. And today, behind the tree...

She would never be able to explain how much it had meant to have his arms around her. He'd made her feel that all would be well, even though she had never cried like that before. Even though that scent of pine had reminded her of that long-ago hurt. He'd helped her, at the cost of his personal embarrassment. It was only fair that she try to advance his cause.

As she sat next to her mother, embroidering her tablecloth, her mind kept shying back to Grantham.

"Mother," she said, finally, "what do you know of Grantham?"

"You're going on a few house calls with him, aren't you? Is there any interest there?"

Lydia colored. "No, no. Of course not." She wasn't so foolish as to become interested in a man who wanted another. Even if she *did* want to know who it was.

Her mother looked at her for a long while, until Lydia dropped her eyes. There wasn't any interest on her part. Just...curiosity, that was all. She wanted to know what sort of woman would capture the imagination of that sort of man.

He was singularly straightforward. His regard would be a compliment in a way that another man's would not. He wouldn't be the sort to imagine a girl perfect because he was confused by his physical desire. He would see her—all her faults—and would decide that he wanted her anyway. Lydia simply wanted to know who this paragon was who had earned his affection.

Whoever it was, she had to be pretty. He wouldn't have made a list of pretty women if he didn't value the characteristic. Maybe it was Joanna Perkins. She was absolutely lovely, with that bright golden hair and that brilliant laugh. He'd like a woman who laughed—they could laugh together.

But he'd said he'd paid her marked attention, and she could not recall Grantham once walking with Miss Perkins and courting that laugh of hers. She tried to remember seeing him talking to another woman. He was so tall that he would have to bend to murmur sweet nothings.

That mental image—the idea of Grantham leaning over another woman the way he had with Lydia today, giving her that dark, wicked smile that seemed meant for her alone—that made her fists clench in a way that she didn't care to examine. She would have remembered seeing him talk to another woman that way. She couldn't have helped but remember it.

Maybe he was more circumspect than she'd imagined. She'd tell him that tomorrow that he needed to be more marked in his affections.

Her father had joined her mother today. They sat next to each other, she embroidering, he reading through a list of reports, his spectacles perched on the end of his nose.

"What do you think of Grantham?" Her heart raced as she spoke.

Her father looked over the rims of his spectacles at her. "Am I going to have to have another talk with him?"

"No. No. I'm just accompanying him on a few house calls." And hitting him, and bursting into tears, and letting him hold her. And then there were the topics of their conversation. Safe to say that she wouldn't tell her father that Grantham was instructing her on the use of French letters. He might take that amiss.

Lydia looked up at the ceiling. "He's an interesting man. I only want to figure him out."

"Hmm," her father said. He glanced over at her mother, who gave him a repressive shake of her head.

Grantham had said she could figure out who it was, and Lydia wouldn't be able to sleep until she did. It couldn't be that he'd been in love with *Minnie,* could it? Lydia's best friend had married recently, and it would make perfect sense if he liked her. She was intelligent and beautiful—perhaps not the kind of beauty that would land on lists, but the kind that anyone with eyes could see, if only they looked long enough. It would explain why he hadn't said a word. Lydia could have ceded him to Minnie without even thinking.

Except...

Except that up until two months ago, Minnie hadn't had a decent prospect at all, and she'd been near the point of desperation. Grantham would have had only to speak the word, and she would have been his.

Not Minnie.

Doctor Grantham had told her that he had a few defects in his character.

Lydia knew she had a few faults of her own, and one of the things she knew she was shockingly good at was telling lies to herself. She had convinced herself she would be happy to marry a man she didn't care for, simply because it made sense to marry him and would have done her father good. She'd convinced herself that there was *something else* that would happen when she married—something besides the unholy joining of male and female forms, something beside the emission of seed, simply because the man she loved had said it was so.

She'd convinced herself that she wasn't angry about what had happened to her. Lydia knew that she lied to herself as assiduously as Grantham told the bare truth.

But occasionally, she managed to shock even herself.

She had just thought to herself that she could have *ceded* him to her friend. As if the mere fact that he'd held her this afternoon meant that he belonged to *her*. She didn't want him for herself, did she? She couldn't want him. He was... He was...

Lydia swallowed.

He was in love with another woman.

She knows, she remembered him saying calmly. *I am not a particularly subtle individual.*

"Oh," she said aloud, "you sly little...sneaky...ridiculous..."

She ran out of insults just as her parents both looked up at her.

"Not you," she said to her father. "Not you either, Mother."

But he hadn't been sly or sneaky. He'd been remarkably upfront. He'd told her that he was madly in love with her, that he had been for months. And he'd said it just sarcastically enough that she'd shook her head and refused to think about the flutter in her belly. It didn't make any sense, though. He couldn't be in love with her. Why, he knew that she'd been pregnant—that she'd had relations with another man outside of marriage.

The hymen is just a membrano-carneous structure...

Oh, God. If she started with the premise that he wanted her, this whole wager took on an entirely different complexion.

If she started with the premise that he wanted her, she didn't even know if she could talk to him. Their easy conversation of the last day, their friendship, his jokes about gonorrhea... The way he'd put his arms around her and held her, even when doing so had made the circumstance of his physical arousal so apparent. Everything had been so simple.

I may be difficult, but I am remarkably constant in my affections, and I have thought of her every day for these last sixteen months.

He was talking about *her.* He'd been talking about her the whole time. He'd known it and he'd looked straight at her and said those things, knowing precisely what he was saying and who he was saying it to.

And he was right. She'd known it. Even when she had been unable to admit it in her mind, her body had known, inclining to his, molding to his. She'd thrilled when he'd looked at her. That was neither fear she felt nor antipathy. That shock that traveled through her when he looked at her...that was attraction.

Lydia swallowed.

She should have been happy at the discovery. She was beginning to like him—perhaps more than like him. To realize that he felt the same way about her, that he'd been so fixed on her despite all the things she'd said to him...

No. The *last* thing she needed was this *want,* this feeling that he might complete her in a way that everyone else could not. The last thing she needed was to flush when he talked of sexual arousal, to have him tell her in that calm way that it was natural, normal. That she could have it, that it wasn't wrong.

If she didn't acknowledge what she felt, what he wanted, then it couldn't lead her astray. She wanted to turn away and bury her head in her skirts. She wanted to take that certainty and stuff it back where she'd hid it before. But there was no way to unknow the thing she didn't want to know. He wanted her, and she wanted him back.

Knowledge led to action; action led to heartbreak.

She knew, now, and she wished she didn't.

Chapter Ten

S<small>HE KNEW.</small>

Jonas could tell from the way she no longer met his eyes, the way she wouldn't take his arm this afternoon. He could tell by the way she scarcely answered him when he spoke to her on the way to their final destination. And he could most particularly tell because when he guided her into the house far down Fosse Street, when he brought her close to him and led her through the labyrinth of rubbish that made up the front room, she drew away from him as soon as they reached the hob in back.

"You should go on ahead of me," he said.

"But—"

"He's expecting you," Jonas told her. "I told him the other night that you would be here, and you can rest assured that he was delighted by the prospect of a visit from a pretty girl. He wouldn't hurt you, even if he could."

He looked around the room at the chaos that always reigned here, and felt a full-blown body itch settle into his skin. "I have a few things to do down here first." Such as washing his hands and wrapping that end of cheese in wax paper. Such as avoiding the fact that he'd intended to introduce Lydia to his father.

When she hesitated, he said, "You're welcome to stay down here. Alone with me."

And of course, on that, she went up without him. He washed the teapot and found a bucket for water.

"Call me Lucas," he could hear his father saying, as Jonas slipped out the door and headed to the pump.

By the time he got back and put some water on the hob to boil, they were chattering like old friends. He couldn't quite make out their conversation over the clank of the dishes as he scrubbed them out. Trust Lydia to charm his father in a quarter of an hour.

He snorted.

Trust his father to charm Lydia as well. He gathered up tea things on a tray—all clean now, the silver shining and the teapot whiter than it had been in years—and started up the stairs.

"I do want some explanation," Lydia was saying. "What *is* all of this?"

Jonas could hear the note of distaste in her voice, could imagine her gesturing to the piles of rubbish alongside his bed.

"This is my independence." Just as easily, he could hear the pride in his father's voice. "I don't mean to be a burden on my son in my old age," his father said. Pride. Overwhelming pride.

Granthams don't cry, he remembered his father telling him when he was eleven. *So you're going back to school, and I won't hear any more complaints from you. No matter what they do to you.*

"Does your son think of you as a burden?"

"He's just starting out in life," his father said earnestly. "About to get married, he is. He doesn't want an old man leaning on him. When I'm back on my feet, I'll be able to cut this all up for the scrap metal." Jonas came up the last few stairs, just in time to see his father lean in. "You see this? Everyone thinks it's junk. But what you can see right now may well be worth ninety-five pounds. You hear that? Ninety-five pounds, if you know what to do with it."

That last was delivered in the kind of voice that an elderly man believed to be a whisper, but which could have been heard three counties over.

To her credit, Lydia didn't guffaw. "Ninety-five pounds," she said quietly. "My, that's clever of you."

"Clever. Ha. I'm not the clever one. You know my son. Now, *there's* a clever boy. When he was three, I said to his mother—this boy is going to be something, if only we don't get in his way. The local grammar school wasn't good enough for him, no. We knew we had to get him into Rugby. Not easy for a scrap-metal dealer, do you think?"

She made an appropriately appreciative noise. Neither of them had seen him, standing in the shadows of the stairwell, simply drinking in the sight of them together.

"If there was a penny to be squeaked, my wife squeaked it," his father announced proudly. "And what she didn't save, I found. And after she...well, never mind that. My son, he went from Rugby to King's College. Worked with them over on Portugal Street for a few years, he did."

"You must be very proud," Lydia said.

"Well, that's as might be. Right now, I just want to know, where the devil is the—" He turned toward the stairwell and caught sight of Jonas standing there. All that proud boasting closed in on itself. He folded his skinny arms and looked down. "Took you long enough," he grumbled.

It had ever been like that between them. For years, Jonas had thought that his father was gruff, that he could never please him. It had taken him until early adulthood to understand that his father was proud—so proud that his pride shamed him.

Jonas set the stacked cup and saucers on the bedside table, distributed them, and poured the tea.

He handed Lydia her cup. "There's no cream or sugar, unfortunately. It's not good for his heart."

"As if I would in any event. Did you know the average man spends one pound six shillings a year on sugar, if you add it all up? I read it the other day. Over the course of a man's life, that adds up to well over sixty pounds. Just for having a little sweetener. You seem a sensible woman, Miss Charingford. You don't take sugar, do you?"

"A little."

"Two sugars. And cream." Jonas had watched her often enough.

"Two sugars?" His father looked scandalized. "Why, that's a hundred-pound habit. Best to break it now. But do you know what this fellow has me doing?" He gestured at Jonas.

Lydia shook her head.

"I've told him a thousand times that if you mix lard with rice, you can scarcely taste the difference between that and meat. Can you believe he's had the temerity to instruct the grocers not to send me any more lard?"

Lydia's eyes only widened a fraction at that. She blinked a few times, but then managed to answer. "I can believe it," she said. "He is a most officious man, when he puts his mind to it. But..." She glanced once at Jonas, and then looked away. "But I do think he means well," she whispered.

"ARE WE STILL PRETENDING THIS IS ABOUT A WAGER?" Lydia asked, as they left his father's home.

He looked over at her. "There is a wager on the table. And if I win, I still intend to collect." The last thing he wanted, though, was to *win*.

She looked away. "I have no idea what you're doing." Her voice was quiet. She threaded her fingers together, looking down. "You could have shown me a great deal worse than you have. You aren't even trying to win. I don't know what you want."

She still hadn't looked at him.

"I think, Lydia," he said carefully, "that you do know."

She shook her head furiously. "I don't," she insisted. "You can't want me to say that I see nothing good about that old man. That's ridiculous. He's not well, and his mind seems...not what it might once have been. I surmise that his house is the cause of Henry's injury, and I could weep for that. But the pride in his eyes when he talked of his son, his sense of familial feeling... There is love there. And that means I win the wager." Her fists balled. "I win, and you don't care, and I don't understand you."

"There is only one thing you don't understand," Jonas said quietly. "I didn't intend to ask you if you found something good in the man we visited today. There is a great deal that is good in him. I wanted to ask you what you thought of his son."

That stopped her in her tracks. She frowned. "His son?"

"His son. That's all I've ever wanted to discover. How you felt about his son."

"But..." She swallowed.

"Let me tell you a little about the family before you proceed," Jonas said. But he didn't think he could finish this, not on the public streets. Instead, he put his hand in the small of her back and led her across the street to the park.

In the last day, the tree had been trimmed. Little metal candleholders graced the ends of the branches. Snowflakes made of quills and goose feathers nestled among the greenery, and a gold ribbon had been threaded around it. As he came closer, he could smell the orange-and-clove of constructed pomanders mixing with the smell of fresh pine.

"Are you well acquainted with the family?"

"You might say that," he said, guiding her to the tree. He left her standing at the edge of the stage. He himself leaped up and examined the ornaments. It gave him something to do other than look in her eyes.

"As you may have surmised," he said, "Lucas was born poor. He was the sixth son of a costermonger, one who learned only the rudiments of reading and writing. He started buying and selling scrap-metal, rummaging through middens to find bits that he could trade. He saved every penny he could and worked arduously to build not just a living, but a thriving business. He married late in life—it had taken him several decades to build himself up. Even after he married, his wife had a difficult time having children. His only child was born after twelve years of marriage; his wife died five years later. Lucas was solely responsible for his son from that point on."

There were painted angels made of tin hidden within the branches of the tree, angels that would reflect the light of the candles once they were lit. He supposed a tree wasn't the worst of traditions.

"I would wager he was a good father," Lydia said, coming up on the stage to stand by him, and Jonas felt a twinge.

"A very good father." Jonas's throat closed, and he leaned in to look at a bugle of frosted glass. "Strict, mind you, and frugal, but he made sure his son got a good education. And when the parish teacher came to him and told him that his son had a real talent for learning, he..."

A little string of bells hung on the tree, and a passing breeze made them ring lightly. It reminded him of his father waking him on Christmas with bells, making the holiday feel like a large family affair when it had really just been the two of them. That Christmas, his father—his father who thought carefully before purchasing a pair of socks, if the ones he had could possibly be mended—had given him a wildly extravagant gift.

Jonas swallowed. "He didn't hesitate to purchase his son an expensive set of encyclopedias. That from the man who once picked horseshoe nails off the street, who refuses sugar to save a few shillings every week. Another man might have insisted that his son take over his business; instead, when he found out that his son had the chance go to university, if only he could find the money... Lucas sold the scrap yard that he'd spent two decades building." The one his father had thought was the beginning of not just a business, but a real empire. "He gave up all that, just for his son."

Lydia looked over at him. "This is the son who allows him to live..."

He breathed in pine and closed his eyes. "This is the son who lets him live in that pile of refuse," Jonas told her. "That very one."

Her eyes grew shadowed. "I suppose he has become a barrister or some other sort of important individual."

"I suppose he has."

"And he no longer has time for his father," she said sadly. "He cannot have visited, not since...not since all this started. Or he would never have allowed it to happen."

Jonas let out a long breath and forced himself to turn to her. "He visits," he said softly. "He visits every day. But he is at a loss as to what to do with him. He's tried to have the wreckage forcibly cleared, but...the last time he attempted it, the constables were called. He's afraid his father will work himself into an apoplexy if he tries again. At this point, his only option is to have his own father—the father who sacrificed everything to make him what he is—declared incompetent, his house cleared by force, and his father sedated during the whole process so that he does himself no injury. What kind of son does such a thing?" He balled his hands into his fists. "What kind of son does nothing? I fear for his heart, if he were to be removed from those surroundings. I fear for his health, if he stays." He took a long, shaking breath. "My God, Lydia, I wish you would tell me what you think about his son."

Her eyes met his. He wasn't sure how long she'd known, at what point in the story she had figured out the truth. Hell, when he started talking, he hadn't been sure if she knew at all. His father might have made it plain in their conversation, before Jonas came up with the tea things.

She took a step toward him. "His name is Lucas...Grantham?"

A single, short nod.

"You didn't tell me you were taking me to see your father."

"No." He looked away. "I didn't. I told him I was bringing you to see him, though." He smiled. "He gave you his lard-and-rice receipt, which is proof positive that he likes you. He only mentions that to people he approves of. And don't worry about the sugar in your tea. He hates when I take sugar, too."

It was all babble. He couldn't look away from her. She was standing in front of him, looking up at him.

"You want me to tell you what I think of you." She took another step toward him.

"I wanted to spend time with you, to convince you I wasn't the ogre you feared." He looked away. "Little did I know that over the course of these last days, I'd learn more of you, too. That you were brave. That beneath your laughter and your cheer, there lies a solid measure of good sense." He swallowed. He was babbling still. "You make me happy. And what I most keenly want to know is... Do you think I could ever do the same for you?"

She put her finger on his lips. "Jonas."

His Christian name sounded awkward on her lips. It was the first time he'd heard her say it. The smell of pine was strong. He couldn't look away from her. She set her hands on his arms—the curls that hung at her cheeks brushed his jaw. She stood so close, he could almost taste her. She stepped closer still. Jonas bent to her, tasting the sweetness of her breath. Her lips were dizzyingly close. And then...

She kissed him.

Oh, God. For one moment, he was riveted in place by that single, solitary point of contact. Her lips on his—how long had he envisioned this moment? Long enough that he let his eyes flutter shut, let himself fall into the feel of it. That light caress, the brush of her lips against his...

He'd have called it bittersweet, but all the sweetness came from her, the bitterness from him. Her kiss didn't sweep away the dark anguish he felt in his heart. Instead, it embraced it. It acknowledged it. *This is real,* her kiss said, *your hurt is real. It is real and important. So let me share it with you.*

It was a kiss like dark chocolate, a heady mix of cacao and sugar, each ingredient imperfect on its own, but breathtaking when mixed together. And when he tasted her, when he nipped at her lips and she opened up to him, she was sweet and tart, like cherries in brandy.

He wrapped his arms around her and kissed her more deeply. "Lydia." Her name was perfect on his lips, perfect whispered against hers.

And God, she knew how to kiss. A man could fall into a kiss like this and never want to leave. Her body molded itself to his, giving up all its secrets. The warm flush of her chest as she slid more deeply into sexual arousal; the perk of her nipples, felt only dimly through the layers of fabric between them. Her hips pressed against his, acknowledging his growing arousal with her own.

He'd wanted a kiss for midwinter. But secretly, he'd wished for this— that she might not only see him, but like him. Maybe love him.

"Jonas," she whispered, opening up for him. He leaned forward and set his hands on the rough plaster to either side of her head. Pine needles tickled his legs, but none of it mattered. He couldn't have been more comfortable in a feather bed surrounded by pillows than he was at this moment.

He wasn't sure when her hands started roaming, when his own moved in response. He only knew that it seemed right to bring his hand to her ribs. He could feel the shape of her corset, the boning, the grommets and laces hidden behind fabric and ribbons. The thick fabric of her undergarment nestled just under her breasts, leaving the shape of her bosom for his exploration. He ran his thumbs along her nipples, until her breath came in gasps, until they hardened to aroused peaks under his touch.

She was so responsive, so passionate. As much as he'd ever imagined, pressing against him, opening her mouth to him, meeting his tongue stroke for stroke.

"Lydia," he said. "Lydia, darling."

On those words her eyes opened. They opened wide. Her breath stuttered out from her in little white puffs. How could it be so cold when he felt so warm?

He struggled for the words to give her.

She pulled away. "No." But he wasn't even sure she was talking to him. "No." She took two steps back.

He felt pole-axed with his own lust.

"Don't tell me this is normal," she said. "It isn't. It *isn't.*"

"Lydia."

She didn't look at him. Her lips were pressed together.

"Lydia," he said. "I want to marry you. I want to have you by my side forever. I know it's far too soon to ask. But, Lydia, darling—"

"Don't call me that." Her voice was shaking. "I don't want to hear it. Not ever again." She put her hands to her head. "Oh, God," she said. "Look at me. Just look at me."

He couldn't take his eyes from her. Even with the tree glistening with new ornaments, she was the most lovely thing around, her lips still pink from their kiss.

"You can't walk away from me after this," he said.

She looked up, and what he saw in her eyes brought him to a standstill. Her eyes were wide, the pupils shrunk to pinpoints.

She took a few steps back. "You're very good," she said. "Very good. I had no intention of... But you made me forget." Her voice shook. "You made me forget what could happen."

"Lydia. It doesn't have to be that way."

He took a step toward her. She flung an arm out at him, pointing, and he halted. "There," she said. "You're honest. You're surprisingly sweet, when you wish to be. And...and I think you could tempt any woman you chose." He'd thought her so sweet just moments before, but there was a bitterness to her voice now. "So I do see good in you. That was the wager, was it not?"

"Hang the wager," he swore.

"You promised," she said. "You promised that if I won, you would never talk to me again."

He swallowed. "Only if that's what you wanted. Lydia, you can't mean to kiss me and then walk away."

"I mean it." Her voice was shaking, and he thought she was on the verge of tears. "I really mean it. I don't want to talk to you ever again."

He took a step toward her. "Lydia."

She flinched back. "Your word," she said. "You gave your word."

But it wasn't the promise he'd made that stopped his tongue. It was the look in her eyes—that black, dark look, that fear that only intensified as he came closer. He shut his mouth, pressing his lips together, searching for something to say...

There was nothing. He'd promised not to speak to her any longer.

"I'm sorry," she said. "I can't. I simply can't."

She backed away from him. And when she was six feet away, she turned and ran, leaving him alone with the evergreen and the ornaments.

Chapter Eleven

THE FIRE IN HER FATHER'S STUDY WAS HOT, but Lydia could scarcely feel it against her skin. She wasn't sure why she'd fled here—why she sat here fiddling with the holly on his desk. She felt empty and hollow, and she didn't *want* to think. Not at all.

"So," her father said, setting down his pen after she rearranged the ribbons for a fourth time, "am I going to have to have words with Grantham after all?"

She jumped back, stricken. "No! Why would you say that? I don't want to talk about him."

He smiled faintly. "I've made three errors in this last column, Lydia, and you haven't caught a single one."

"I have to get this holly right." She didn't look at him.

He didn't say anything. He wasn't the sort to *say* things, to cajole her into giving up her fears. He just…was.

"Why didn't you put me away?" she asked.

His eyes widened.

"You should have. Parwine told you to do it. *Anyone* would have done it in your place. But you act as if nothing happened, as if I were the same person I would be if I'd never met Paggett."

Her father took his glasses and rubbed the bridge of his nose, where the frame of his spectacles had left a pink indentation. But he didn't say anything in response.

"Don't you understand that I'm not your little girl anymore?" she demanded.

"No. You've grown older," he said quietly.

"Grown older? Is that what you think I've done? That's all you think happened to me? That I just *grew older?*"

He gave her a helpless shrug. "Well, yes. I do wish it hadn't happened all at once, the way it did, but…" Another shrug. "I never really thought about putting you away. I suppose almost anyone else would say that was a mistake. But I didn't want to."

"You didn't even give me new rules, no new strictures. You let me walk out with Grantham, knowing that I was the sort of woman who might…"

She didn't finish the answer. She was the sort of woman who might fall prey to a man like that. A darkly handsome man, possessed of a particularly blunt style of speaking. She might let him touch her, kiss her. She might thrill when he did it and want more.

His eyebrows rose. "I ask again, am I going to have to have words with the man?"

"No!"

He gestured with his hand to his desk drawer. "Because if necessary, I could fetch my pistol and—"

"No!" she exclaimed, horrified. "No. But do you remember who he is?"

Her father frowned. "He's a doctor. Is there something else I should know?"

"He was with Parwine. When…"

Her father's face went white. He hadn't known. Her parents had been so focused on *her* on that day that she didn't think they had been aware of anyone else. Lydia had been the one staring across the room, glaring at that strange young man who watched her so silently.

Her father's hand drifted towards his drawer once again. "Is Grantham using what he knows to cause you harm?" His voice was a whisper.

She shook her head. "He wouldn't hurt me." In fact, she was fairly certain she'd hurt him. "He only made me realize—"

He'd only made her realize how much she hurt.

"I don't want to realize anything," she finally said.

Those words sounded awful spoken aloud. They rang out in the quiet of her father's study. Lydia put her fingers to her lips, tentatively, testing to see if they'd come from her.

They had.

"Well, now," her father said. "I guess you know why I didn't put you away. Once you're old enough to punish yourself, there's no point in my doing it, too. And since I wasn't so inclined, I didn't."

THE NEXT FEW DAYS SEEMED TO PASS IN A BLUR. Lydia smiled; she laughed. But she knew it all for lies.

A week before Christmas, she went out for a walk. She wrapped herself heavily, but no scarf, however thick, could keep her memories from her. And with the holiday so close, there was no avoiding those old memories.

Christmas bells reminded her of that long-ago time, the one she tried not to think about. She'd spent years telling herself that it was as if nothing had happened. That she was strong, because she could set aside those months when she'd been so casually used by a man who cared nothing for her. That she had suffered once on that Christmas Eve when everything had gone wrong, but that she'd overcome it. That she'd learned to laugh and smile, and that she had gone on, unharmed by those events.

She'd lied to herself. And she hadn't understood how deep those lies ran.

Because it wasn't until a man had kissed her and called her darling, had said he wanted to marry her, that all those old feelings had come rushing back. It had been as if she were fifteen again, naïve and hopeful, believing everything he said. Letting him touch her. It didn't matter that Jonas had been sincere. It didn't matter how she felt about him. She'd felt her own physical desire sitting on her like a nauseating reminder of what could happen. Her gut had cramped, and she'd run away.

And now…

Now, she didn't even know what she wanted.

At the outdoors market, she smelled the sharp, sweet scent of wassail, cinnamon and orange slices wafting from a pot, and she remembered choking down that bitter solution that Parwine had recommended, not knowing what she was doing. She saw a branch of holly decorating a plate of gingerbread, and she remembered her father trying to put a good face on a holiday where Lydia could only huddle in bed, doubled over from the pain.

There was the mistletoe piled on a market table, a poisonous, parasitic reminder that kisses could lie.

She ducked down a side street, but holiday cheer followed her there, too. Bells rang as doors opened; ivy graced shop windows. Bakeries let off clouds of sweet-smelling spice as people ducked in and out for cinnamon bread. She smiled and wished everyone she saw a happy holiday, but Jonas Grantham had been right. Saying Christmas was happy didn't make it so.

There was only one place that she could find to escape. Down a smaller street, a church waited. Its small, quiet collection of gravestones was the only surcease she found from the unrelenting cheer of the season.

She escaped into the middle of it, and there, with cold stones surrounding her, sat on a bench and wept. For so long, she hadn't let herself feel anything at all. She'd smiled and laughed and ignored the harm that had been done. But deep inside, she hadn't stopped wanting, and no matter how she'd tried, no matter what lies she told herself, she had still hurt.

The little churchyard was isolated, fronted only by a quiet residential street. For minutes, nobody passed; when somebody did, he didn't look her way. She held her breath. No reason for him to look in the yard. No reason for him to look at her at all. He passed the black iron gate in the stone wall.

She caught sight of a black bag, and her breath caught. Any number of gentlemen carried black bags. They were common, and if this one was wider and deeper than usual…

He stopped in his tracks and turned to her.

Oh God, it was Jonas Grantham. She didn't want him to see her now. She didn't want to see him *ever*.

There was no way to hide the tears tracking down her face. Still, she reached hastily for a handkerchief. She wiped her eyes and blew her nose, hoping against hope...

But no; he unlatched the gate and came up the walk. He didn't approach swiftly. He was advancing with all the care of a predator, walking like a cat on a tightrope, one foot in front of the other. And she was too weary to scurry away.

A part of her even welcomed his approach. Maybe he'd look at her and he'd say something outrageous, something that would drive her tears away, allow her to replace this ache inside her with anger.

But he didn't say anything. He stopped in front of her. His eyebrows drew down. He leaned down to her—so close, she could smell a hint of bay rum on his collar.

Even now, he turned her upside down.

He didn't say anything. Of course he didn't; he was still holding to that stupid wager she'd forced on him. Lydia found herself unable to speak as well. Unable to move away.

His eyes met hers. He smiled—not brilliantly, but almost sweetly.

When had she realized that he was sweet? He hid it so well behind gruff speeches, but she'd seen the evidence of it on those days spent with him. The way he talked to Mrs. Hall, setting forth her options so clearly. The way he'd browbeat Henry Westing into accepting an offer of "employment" when he'd been injured and had no other income. The anguish he felt over his father's impossible situation.

Even the way he talked to her. It was outrageous. It was blunt. It was impossible. And it was...precisely what she needed, the truth boned and filleted without garnish or flourish, placed in front of her for her decision. He made her wants seem ordinary instead of dark and dangerous.

He stopped in front of her and bent down. Lydia's breath stopped. He made it seem so uncomplicated to yearn for his touch, so simple to lean into his hand when he set it against her cheek. He ran his thumb under her eye, wiping a tear away before it could slip away. His fingers played against her nose, her mouth. And then, bending just a little further, he touched his lips to hers.

It wasn't a kiss like the one they'd exchanged a few days past, hot and whole-mouthed. It was lighter than that and yet far deeper, a kiss made more of longing than lust. It was the kind of kiss that never happened in fairytales. This wasn't the meeting of lips that woke princesses from a sleep of a hundred years. It wouldn't break enchantments or seduce dark knights from their unholy destinies.

It was the kind of kiss a man might give a princess whose enchantment had been shattered years in the past, a woman who was struggling to understand a world without ensorcellment. His fingers against her cheek acknowledged her deepest hurts, and that made his kiss the subtlest kind of magic.

He straightened, pulling away from her.

"Jonas…" she began.

But he set his finger to his lips in an unmistakable gesture. His eyebrow arched confidently—annoyingly even.

"What are you—"

This time, his hand went over her lips. He smiled at her. And then, he sat next to her and kissed her again, this time harder, his breath hot, melding with hers, his hands taking hold of hers.

Anyone could have seen them there, but she couldn't have pushed him away. He was warm, and she needed the feel of his hands, his lips so dreadfully.

"He used to call me darling," she confessed. "Tom Paggett did. Lydia darling, he'd say, Lydia darling, I can't wait until we marry." She found herself choking on those words. "I wish I were rational like you, but it is hard for me to bear. To hear anyone say those things. It stirs up old memories that I thought I had put to rest."

His hands squeezed hers. He leaned against her.

"I didn't want it to change me. I didn't want to admit that it had any effect on me at all. But it did. It did, and I can't deny it any longer. I used to think that so long as I kept smiling, so long as I never admitted that anything was wrong, it couldn't be. But it was wrong inside me all along."

It was comforting, in a way, to have him keep silent. He didn't offer answers or solutions, just warmth. Strength.

"The truth isn't a gift," she told him. "It's a terror. And every time I look at you, I feel it. I heard a few words from you and scampered away in fear. You scare me. You always have. Feeling that passion again. Feeling that I'm losing myself, giving myself over to another person without any thought as to the consequences."

He gave her another smile, this one wry. He looked upward, briefly, and then shrugged.

"It was an utterly terrible thing for me to do to you. Your father—you must be hurting, wondering what to do about him. Do you know what hurt the most afterward? Not the memories that you brought up, but remembering the look in your eyes as I left. That terrible, cold, lonely look. How could you ever forgive me?"

If he could speak, she suspected he would say something awful right now, something awful and wrong. She suspected he would make her laugh. As it was, her shudders had faded. There was nothing to her world but the warmth of his hands, the way he stroked her shoulder.

"I wish I knew why you were doing this. Being so kind to me."

Without saying a word, he opened his black bag and took out a book. It was labeled carefully on the front: *Visits, 3 September 1863 to...* The end date was blank. He opened it to the middle and then dipped his hand in his bag and came up with a small pair of scissors. This he used to slice a page carefully from the center. He withdrew a pencil and wrote something on the paper, and then, just as carefully, he folded it into a perfect square with crisp edges.

Then he stood. He took her hand, and in perfect silence, slid the paper into it. He closed her fist around it. The corners dug into her palm as he kissed the tips of her fingers. He didn't say anything, not even at that point. He simply turned, picked up his bag, and walked away, leaving Lydia to stare after him, dumbfounded.

It was only after he'd disappeared that she unfolded the page he'd taken from his book.

I only said I would stop talking to you, he'd written. *I never promised to stop loving you.*

She stared at those words, strong and steady, unmoving. It was a strange feeling, accepting that—that she hadn't destroyed everything, that despite everything she'd done, he cared for her still.

It scared her, the truth. The truth was... She liked him. The truth was, ever since the beginning, she'd looked at him and felt that shower of sparks in her belly. He made her feel so carnally *aware*, and so she'd pushed him away as hard as she could.

She sat on the bench for a half-hour, this time recalling everything she knew of him. The straightforward way he'd described prophylactics, not flinching at using words like penis or cervix.

As if carnal exercise and sexual longing were just...things. Regular things, functions of the body, and no cause for embarrassment. As if desire, like the truth, could be a gift and not just a source of shame and terror.

Lydia had told him once that she could let herself see both the good and the bad about a situation. Here was the bad: Maybe she was irretrievably damaged, unable to love normally, unable to accept the regard of a good man because of what had happened in her past.

Or maybe...maybe she was on the brink of love, if only she could let herself accept it.

She remembered the conversation she'd overheard between Jonas and her father. *Your daughter is stronger than you think,* he'd said.

She'd been wrong about him. Apparently, he could hope for the best, too.

Maybe he was right. Maybe she was stronger than she'd thought.

Chapter Twelve

"So," LUCAS GRANTHAM SAID, SITTING UP AND COUGHING. "What do you think? Another few weeks until I'm well again?"

Jonas wiped off his stethoscope and stored it in his bag. He'd told his father the truth all too many times over the last year, and not once had the man listened. The truth no longer fit inside his father's brain.

"Father," he said quietly, "I was hoping you would come home with me."

Lucas Grantham's jaw jutted out and he glowered. "Don't want to be a burden. Never going to be a burden to you."

This was the man who had made him go back to school, even when the other boys teased. His father had taken good care of him, cajoling him and treasuring him in turns. And now...now it was his turn.

"You won't be a burden," Jonas whispered. He looked up and away. He thought of the flesh on his father's legs, pitted with edema, feeling more and more like firm clay as fluid collected there. Evidence of a large heart slowly coming to a halt. He could hear his father's breath, shallower, more rasping now than it had been even a week ago.

"I'm going to ask Miss Charingford to marry me," he said simply. "Next year, I'll spend Christmas with her." God, he hoped he would. "These days, everyone is interested in the new customs, but you taught me about the old. About how to spend Christmas Day without spending a great deal of money. I want to make sure that I have that with her. So I thought that maybe, this Christmas...maybe you could come stay with me for a space of time."

His father frowned and considered this.

"There are so many things I don't remember. You'll have to tell me them all. I don't want to do this wrong. Stay for a few weeks. Just until you're well again." His voice caught at that, and he forced himself to look over at the wall. A few weeks until his father was well. If he had any luck, it would be more than a few weeks—and his father wouldn't notice the passing of those months any more than he saw the time passing now.

"But my things," Lucas Grantham said, looking about him. "If I go, who will watch my things?"

"I'll send over a locksmith. He can make another lock for the door, so you'll know that your things will be safe until you're well again. I promise I won't move a single box. We'll leave a note on the door, for people who come around with things to sell, letting them know that you'll be back soon."

This was met with a frown. "Just for a little while?"

Jonas smiled sadly. "Just for a little while. Only until you're better."

His father looked around the room blankly, searching for a reason to stay, looking for something to hold to in this rubbish-filled room.

"Please," Jonas said. "Father. I need you to do this for me. I need you to do this more than I've ever needed you to do anything."

His throat felt sore and scratchy.

Senility had robbed his father of most of his mind, almost all his dignity. But there was one thing that hadn't yet been taken.

"You...you need me to be with you?" his father asked, his voice wavering.

"I do."

The man who had bought those beautiful leather-bound encyclopedias looked around him. The man who had sold an entire business to give his son a future hadn't disappeared entirely. He leaned over the edge of the bed and picked up the handle of a pan. He frowned at it, shook his head, and then looked up.

"Very well," he said. "But I'll choose the lock, and it will be a proper thick one. And I will have the only key, mind you, and I'll wear it around my neck."

"Of course," Jonas said. He leaned over and took his father's hand in his. "Of course. And just as soon as you're well..."

But he couldn't make himself finish the sentence. These next months wouldn't be easy. But now, for the first time, he could see his way through them. He sat on the edge of the bed, holding his father's wrist, feeling the pulse of the man who had given life to him.

It beat, tired but steady, and Jonas let out a sigh of relief.

BY THE TIME JONAS CAME BACK TO HIS OWN HOME that evening, he was exhausted. It had been a day of many house calls—eight in all, the last one interrupting his dinner. Interspersed between them, he'd managed to engage the services of a locksmith for the next day, and to hire a few men to move the things his father would need for his journey.

He'd not had a moment to himself to think of anything other than work, and given the state of emotional fatigue he found himself in, it was all to the best. His housekeeper had gone by the time he let himself in the front door, and the maid who answered his door had gone to her parents' home back in Nottingham for the holidays. The house was dark and empty. He made his way to the back, where his dinner—now cold—had been laid under a dome. Potatoes, beef, and peas were prosaic enough. He ate methodically, while making notations in his visit log.

By the time it was ten o'clock, he'd cleaned his plate and had finished recording his thoughts for the day. He'd shed his coat, and replaced his shoes and stockings with slippers. He was on the verge of finding his way into bed when a knock came at the door.

For a moment, he stared wearily at the table. The last thing he wanted—the very last thing—was to stand up and go answer that knock. But it was urgent if someone had come at this hour of the night. He was needed. It didn't matter how tired he was. He could sleep later.

He stood and made his way to the door.

A solitary cloaked figure stood there. For a moment, he stared blankly. And then—

Lydia. Because of that wager, he wasn't even able to speak her name aloud. He thought it instead. He felt it with his whole body.

"I'm so sorry for coming at this hour," she whispered, "but I had to wait for my parents to go to sleep."

He looked around, but nobody else was about. And ultimately, his was the one door where a visitor in the night would not be remarked upon.

He could feel his weariness sliding from him. He opened the door wider and gestured her inside.

She hadn't said he could speak, and so he didn't. Not because he felt bound by the wager, but because… Because she needed to choose him at her own pace. To understand that he was willing to wait for her. And he wanted to know that she would choose him over her own dark fears.

He wasn't going to talk, but he helped her take off her cloak, running his hands over her shoulders as he did. He could almost feel the aching tension in his head slip away as his fingers brushed her skin. He hung her cloak on a hook.

When he turned back to her, she faced him. She was holding a gift in one hand—a small sack of gold velvet tied with a green ribbon. It was a ridiculously elaborate presentation, and he couldn't help but smile at it. Ribbons at ten at night? Only Lydia.

She held it out to him. "I brought you a Christmas present." She looked down. "And yes, I know the decoration doesn't change the contents, but it amused me to make it pretty."

No, Lydia would never bring him a package wrapped in brown paper and tied with twine. He wouldn't want her any other way.

He took the package.

"You should open it now."

Bemused, he undid the ribbon. It took several minutes to figure out the complicated bow she'd made. He folded it carefully, and then opened the sack. Inside, he felt the crinkle of paper. He pulled it out. For a second he thought that she'd given him a note—a note to match the one he'd written for her earlier that day. But then he rubbed it between his fingers and realized that this wasn't paper all the way through. It was…

He unfolded the paper and swallowed.

She'd given him a French letter. How in the hell had she found a French letter? He could not mistake the intent in that.

He let out a shaky breath and looked over at her. Her eyes were dark, dark. She reached up and pulled two pins from her hair, and her curls tumbled over her shoulders.

Ever so slowly, he held out his hand to her. Just as slowly, she set her fingers on his. "I would have had Mrs. Hall get me a Dutch cap instead," she said. "But I believe I have to be fitted for one, and, ah…" Her fingers curled around his, and she moved closer to him. "I wanted you to do that."

She stood so close to him now. His entire body yearned for hers.

"I am afraid," she said quietly. "I am afraid because I like you. Because I think back on our conversations and smile. I am afraid because when I see you, my heart beats faster. The truth terrifies me, and the truth, Jonas, is that I want you carnally."

Oh, God. He'd never thought to hear those words from her.

"And in other ways."

He was riveted by her lips, that dusky rose that demanded his touch.

"I think," she said, "that if you could talk right now, you'd offer to marry me first. You'd wait until you laid all my fears to rest before taking me to bed. But I don't want to cosset my fears any longer, Jonas."

As she spoke, he felt his pulse pick up. His body grew tense—not with the aching, painful tension that he'd felt in his shoulders before she'd arrived, but with a warm anticipation. He smiled at her, long and slow.

"I want to face what I fear," she said, and then swallowed. "Tonight."

For an answer, he picked her up in his arms. She let out a little gasp, but he pulled her close and she hooked her arms about his neck. For one moment, she leaned her forehead against his. For one moment, they traded air, their lungs seeming to work in tandem. And then he kissed her.

This time, there was no bitter to the kiss, just light sweetness, a sweetness that built with every caress they traded.

He wasn't sure how he made it to his bedroom, kissing her, holding her, wanting her. As soon as he was inside, he undid the laces of her gown, pushing it down over her shoulders. She stepped out of it—and then smiled as he shook it and hung it on a hook in his wardrobe.

"Really, Jonas?" she asked.

He spread his hands, and crooked a finger. She came toward him and undid the buttons of his waistcoat. "You know," she said, "I was always so intimated by your great height. There's something about being tall that gives a man an unnatural advantage." She took off his waistcoat, looked at him… and then winked at him before folding it carefully.

God, he loved her. He couldn't quite believe she was here, that she was touching him, *wanting* him. She slid a finger in the waistband of his trousers and then pulled the tails of his shirt out. When she ran her hands up his bare abdomen, he let out a gasp. She gave him a scandalous smile, one that brought his blood to a slow simmer. He took off his shirt, carefully, and set it atop his vest. And then, before she could get those wicked fingers on the waistband of his trousers, he undid the laces of her front-facing corset. It peeled away, leaving her in chemise and drawers.

From here, lit by the flickering light of oil lamp, he could see the devastating silhouette of her body. The curves of her hips, the weight of her breasts, no longer supported by her corset. He could see the shading of a dark triangle of hair through the thin fabric of her drawers, the darker points of her nipples. His whole body pulsed with need, the desire to press against hers.

"You're distinctly good at that," she said, a note of amusement in her voice. "But I suppose you'd have to be. If you needed to treat someone in a rush…"

He shook his head.

"No? You didn't learn to remove women's clothing through your profession?"

He crossed the room to his desk, and took a letter opener off his desk.

"Jonas?"

He turned back to her, a smile on his face. What he wanted to say was that when he was in a rush—if minutes had made the difference between life and death—he wouldn't have bothered with laces. But since she hadn't given him leave to speak yet, he'd have to show her. He stalked up to her, hooked his finger in the neckline of her chemise. She just had a moment to look up at him in confusion, before he set the letter opener against the fabric and sliced it clean through.

That. That was what he would do in a rush, if he needed to get at something. Her skin pebbled in the night air, but not for long.

She gasped. And then he pushed her on the bed, the two halves of her chemise falling to either side of her. He dragged her drawers down, baring her body for him. Her eyes were wide, so wide, and dark. She hadn't said a word of protest, and so he spread her legs.

She'd said she wanted him carnally.

Before she could think, he set his lips on her sex in a full-mouthed kiss.

Her hips jerked under his tongue. Her hands found his hair. "Oh my God, Jonas," she gasped. He kissed lightly at first, licking at the edges until her breath stuttered, until he tasted the liquid of her arousal. Then he deepened the kiss, licking up the length of her, finding the hard nub of her clitoris with his tongue.

"Jonas," she said, "Jonas. That feels so—so—"

He couldn't speak, and right now, he didn't want to. He lost himself in the feel of her, the taste of her, her legs clasping around his shoulders, her hands on his scalp. Her sex underneath him, open for him, open for his taste, his tongue. She was open for him to bring her pleasure, and he brought it on her bit by bit, until she trembled beneath him, until she begged incoherently. Until he could taste the edge of her desire, until there was only want in her and no fear.

God, it felt so good. So damned good, just to feel her on his lips, to feel that trembling wave pass through her as she screamed, her back arching, her whole body flushing pink and warm with the orgasm.

He sat back on his heels, grinning.

Slowly, she propped herself up on elbow and looked at him. "You," she said, "are a man of hidden talents." She crooked her finger at him. He stood and walked to her. Her fingers at his waistband—brushing the head of his erect penis—had him gasping. She undid the buttons and slid his trousers down, waiting for him to step over them before setting them neatly with the rest of his clothing. He wished he could make this moment last forever—this moment where she reached out and slid her fingers down him, sending a shiver of sensation through him. Instead, he handed her the French letter.

And when she bit her lip, he showed her what to do with it.

When it was on, she looked up at him. "Make love to me, Jonas," she said.

He joined her on the bed, wrapped his arms around her, and kissed her. He kissed her until her breath came in stuttering gasps, until her limbs trembled under his. Then he spread her legs, set the head of his penis against her vulva, and slid inside her. She was wet around him, wet and tight and so good. So, so good. So good to be seated inside her. To have her breasts to hand, her lips close enough to kiss. So good to thrust, unbearably sweet, into her. To have her arch up into him, gasping, as he took her.

After all this time, he had to bite his lip to keep himself from spilling his seed too soon. But she was already deeply aroused. Every thrust brought a moan from her; every circle of his hips had her moaning. And when he found her nipple with his finger and rolled it around, her vagina clamped around him and another orgasm swept through her.

God, she felt so good around him. So good. So damned good. He came in a great rush.

Afterward—after he'd pulled out, after he'd gathered her up and given her a thousand little kisses, after they'd held each other in laughing wonder...

"There are twelve days of Christmas, yes?" he asked. "Keep the turtle doves and the partridges. This was lovely. Let's do it again."

She sat up and very, very slowly, she smiled. "You cheat. I didn't say you could talk yet."

"I'm no expert," he said, "but I think that when you screamed my name for the second time, it counted as tacit permission."

"You and your technicalities." But she only leaned against him, running her hand along his hip. "I suppose you want French letters instead of French hens? That's not very romantic of you." But she kissed him as she spoke.

"There is really nothing less romantic than chickens," he told her. "They leave droppings all over the place, die at the slightest provocation, and are stupid enough to spend three weeks trying to hatch rocks. You keep your chickens. Let me have my true love, and hang the gifts."

She let out a little breath, ducked her head and put it against his shoulder.

"Lydia." He pulled her close, breathed in the scent of her.

"I need your advice." She spoke without looking up, her breath whispering against his skin.

"Mm."

"There's this man. He's had his eye on me for months, but I haven't always treated him kindly." Her words faltered. "He gave me the truth for Christmas. The first time—and the second time—and the third time he offered it, I couldn't take it. How do I let him know…" Her voice faltered. "How do I let him know that I want nobody but him?"

"Show up in the middle of the night with a French letter," he advised, setting a finger under her chin, "and he'll likely get the message."

He tilted her face up. She looked in his eyes, and he smiled. "No point in being subtle."

"No," she breathed. "I suppose not."

"But just to be sure," he said, leaning down and setting his forehead against hers, "you'd better try it again tomorrow. And the day after. And every day you can, until we're married. When do you think that will be, Lydia? Because I'm hoping for soon. Very soon."

Epilogue

Some weeks later

THERE WAS AN UNEARTHLY LIGHT IN THE ROOM when Lydia woke up that morning—that curious reflected brightness filtering through a gap in the curtains, one that suggested that there was now a foot of snow on the ground.

She sat up, leaned over, and touched her fingers to her husband's shoulder.

Her *husband*. Now, that was a word that was still new, so new that she bit her lip even thinking it. That word was almost as new as the year.

"Jonas," she whispered.

He didn't respond. She could tell he was awake, though, because his eyes screwed shut, and his mouth contorted in a half-grimace.

"Jonas," she repeated, "it *snowed* last night."

"Mmm."

"That means that Minnie and Robert will be trapped here until the trains are running," Lydia said, "and that we can meet them for breakfast after all." Her best friend had come into town for the wedding, and had stayed for almost a week. It had been wonderful, even if Minnie had made a few sly comments along the lines of *I told you he fancied you.* Lydia had been too happy to protest. And, well, Minnie *had* told her so.

"Your hands are cold," Jonas muttered. And before she could say anything in response, he reached out and took her fingers off his shoulder, and then pressed them between his palms. "Let me warm them for you." He held them for a few moments, rubbing them lightly, before opening his eyes. "That's scarcely helping. You know what you need?" he asked.

"What do I need?"

"Increased blood flow," he responded smoothly.

Lydia leaned over and kissed him. "Increased blood flow is my favorite," she informed him, and then proceeded to show him precisely how much she favored proper circulation. Somewhere, in the middle of a long, lingering kiss, he took off her night rail, and she divested him of the remainder of his clothing.

The rest was a foregone conclusion—the warmth of his skin, the slick desire of her own female liquid, and the hard thrust of his body into hers, slow and steady, his hips claiming hers as he looked into her eyes. He was her husband of just a few days, but he already knew how to drive her to the edge of wildness and beyond.

When he'd finished, he kissed her again. "Did I ever tell you why I wanted to marry?" he asked.

"Because you couldn't resist me."

"Because I wanted a source of regular sexual intercourse, one that wouldn't risk disease," he responded.

Lydia leaned into his shoulder, smiling against his skin. "Oh, too bad," she said in mock sympathy. "And instead, you got a wife who loves you."

A smile spread across his face—a big, golden smile, one that had Lydia smiling in return. "There is no instead," he said. "Only *in addition*. I got the woman I loved."

Author's Note

I'VE ALWAYS BEEN FASCINATED by the history of medicine, but I don't think I could have written a doctor before the mid-Victorian era. That's because, for the most part, doctors before then knew so little about the causes of health—and had so few tools available to them for the testing of pharmaceuticals—that it's quite possible that they killed as many patients as they cured. That may be a charitable assessment.

The Semmelweis study Jonas cites in this novella about the correlation between hand-washing after an autopsy and childbed fever was in fact conducted. Sadly, many doctors of the time reacted to this study with outrage. They were furious that someone suggested that they needed to wash their hands, and even angrier that it was implied that they themselves could be the cause of the disease. Semmelweis was so ostracized by the response that he ended up in a madhouse.

As for the prussic acid/cyanide prescribed by Doctor Parwine in the beginning, I am, alas, not making this up, either. (In fact, if you ever think that there's some screwy element of medical stuff that happens in here, trust me—I'm not making it up.) I went looking for a morning-sickness brew that would be a little sketchy, that an older doctor might prescribe in the late 1850s, and got this absolute gem:

Dr. Scellier extols the following mixture, as a remedy for nausea and vomiting, during the period of pregnancy.

Take of lettuce-water, 4 oz—gum arabic, 1 scruple—syrup of white poppies, syrup of marshmallow root, each, 2 oz. —Prussic acid, 4 drops.

— From Colin Mackenzie's *Five Thousand Receipts in the Useful and Domestic Arts,* reprinted in other volumes as late as 1841.

Dr. Scellier luckily only suggested a tablespoon of this every half hour. But this solution is already 100,000 times more toxic than the toxicity for Atlantic salmon listed in the Materials Safety Data Sheet for hydrogen cyanide.

If you're wondering if I made up the lard-and-rice recipe, the answer is—once again—no. I did make one alteration, though. The version I heard sprinkled MSG on top. Mmm, yummy. Thanks to my former roommate Karen for providing that delectable story of cost-saving.

Sometimes I am very grateful to live in the modern world. Right now I am very, very grateful.

Other Books by Courtney

The Brothers Sinister Series
The Governess Affair
The Duchess War
A Kiss for Midwinter— mid-December 2012
The Heiress Effect — 2013
The Countess Conspiracy — 2013

The Turner Series
Unveiled
Unlocked
Unclaimed
Unraveled

The Carhart Series
This Wicked Gift
Proof by Seduction
Trial by Desire

Acknowledgments

I COULDN'T HAVE WRITTEN THIS NOVELLA without Mr. Milan, who happens to be a doctor. He answered every question I could come up with, from questions on the effects of vasoconstriction (Me: If someone's face turns white, would you assume that their capillaries are shrinking? Him: No. I'd make sure they weren't exsanguinating first. Or, me: If you had to take off someone's clothing in a hurry, how would you do it? Him: Scalpel. Me: No, seriously. Him: Given a choice between your pants and your life, which would *you* choose?) to questions on the diagnosis of sexually transmitted disease. Mr. Milan also provided way too much description about what various conditions would look and feel like.

That being said, the only thing that Mr. Milan has in common with Jonas Grantham besides the profession is a tendency to make jokes about sexually transmitted diseases. I would have made Jonas joke about chlamydia (the STD of choice in jokes in the Milan household—I suspect I should rethink saying that my husband and I have an STD of choice, but then, Mr. Milan doesn't read this and doesn't have to know so long as nobody tells him), but it hadn't been discovered yet.

As always, I couldn't have produced this without a team of people who edited, copy-edited, and proofed for me as if I were the only person in the world. My undying thanks to Robin Harders, Anne Victory, and Martha Trachtenberg, who performed miracles. Erica Ridley did a last-minute read and also forced me to go ziplining after I spent a solid week doing nothing but working on this. Maggie Robinson and Elyssa Patrick both read and offered helpful comments.

I'm also deeply thankful to Tessa Dare, Carey Baldwin, and Leigh LaValle, who basically save me from turning into a neurotic, weeping ball of frustration on a regular basis. For everyone else—Pixies, Peeners—thank you for pretending that the answer is "no" when I ask, "Am I insane?"

Thank you, Google Books, for providing medical texts from the era and freaking me out.

And for you—thank you for reading.

Made in the USA
Lexington, KY
23 January 2014